Richard Lee Metcalfe

Life of Vincent Priessnitz

Founder of Hydropathy

Richard Lee Metcalfe

Life of Vincent Priessnitz
Founder of Hydropathy

ISBN/EAN: 9783337059477

Printed in Europe, USA, Canada, Australia, Japan

Cover: Foto ©Raphael Reischuk / pixelio.de

More available books at **www.hansebooks.com**

LIFE OF

VINCENT PRIESSNITZ

FOUNDER OF HYDROPATHY.

By RICHARD METCALFE,

AUTHOR OF
'SANITAS SANITATUM ET OMNIA SANITAS' AND OTHER HYDROPATHIC
WORKS.

PUBLISHED BY
SIMPKIN, MARSHALL, HAMILTON, KENT & CO., LTD.,
4, STATIONERS' HALL COURT, LONDON, E.C.
1898.

Price Five Shillings.

TO COLONEL AND MRS. HANS RIPPER.

I dedicate this sketch of the life of your late father, Vincent Priessnitz, to you.

The profound respect that I have for the memory of Vincent Priessnitz—in whose steps I have been an ardent and devoted follower for forty years—has actuated me as with a sense of duty to make this record of, and to bear my testimony publicly to, his inborn medical genius.

Although the name of Vincent Priessnitz is not widely known in England, you will feel gratified by my assurance that Hydropathy is being increasingly resorted to in England, and that several eminent English medical men recognise its value.

I feel assured that in years to come your father's name will hold a high position amongst the Masters of the art of healing.

R. METCALFE.

' In proportion as any branch of study leads to important and useful results—in proportion as it gains ground in public estimation—in proportion as it tends to overthrow prevailing errors—in the same degree it may be expected to call forth angry declamations from those who are trying to despise what they will not learn, and wedded to prejudices which they cannot defend. Galileo would probably have escaped persecution if his discoveries could have been disproved, and his reasonings refuted.'—DR. WHATELEY.

PREFACE

IN compiling this work, I have been actuated by a desire to do justice to the memory of the founder of the hydropathic system of treating the human body in disease. Although Priessnitz was one of the great benefactors of mankind, and one of the most astounding geniuses of modern times, yet there has been no adequate biography of him published in this country. But his method of healing has been largely followed in England.

On the Continent Priessnitz's name is a household word, and there are hundreds of establishments where the water-cure is carried out on the principles laid down by Priessnitz.

His treatment is recognised by very many members of the medical profession on the Continent, whilst in England the medical profession, with a few notable exceptions, ignores it.

I desire to acknowledge my indebtedness to the biography of Priessnitz by Dr. Selinger for

v

a good deal of detailed information.* This biography was published shortly after the great hydropathist's death. Dr. Selinger was in close terms of intimacy with Priessnitz, and enjoyed his confidence in matters whereon it was his habit to observe silence. As regards the history of the origin of the treatment at Graefenberg, probably no one else could have written it with the fulness Dr. Selinger has.

To Colonel Ripper (of the Austrian Army) Priessnitz's son-in-law, I acknowledge my special indebtedness for many facts, anecdotes, and particulars of treatment, for most of the accompanying illustrations and family portraits, as well as for the unvarying courtesy shown to me during my visit to Graefenberg in 1895.

Vincent Paul Priessnitz, son of the founder of hydropathy, born on June 22, 1847, died very suddenly on June 30, 1884, of heart disease, leaving one son, who attained his majority in June, 1896.

During the period of more than forty years of double trusteeship, Colonel Ripper made numerous and valuable additions to the Graefenberg establishment. He was the chief promoter of the excellent railway communications, which

* Selinger, J. E. M., " Vincenz Priessnitz. Eine Lebensbeschreibung." Mit portrait und facsimile. Wien : Verlag von Carl Gerold und Sohn. 1852. 8vo., pp. viii, and 208 and wrapper.

PREFACE

render Graefenberg easy of access from all quarters, and he added considerably to the accommodation and comfort of visitors.

He extended the network of forest paths, the pride of the locality, and at ·his instigation hundreds of hammocks were placed near these paths in every direction. These hammocks form quite a feature of the place, enabling visitors to remain comfortably out-of-doors for the greater part of the day, to inhale the health-giving air of the pine forests.

Colonel Ripper founded the Sudeten Tourist Association and the Mutual Aid Society of Bath Attendants. He owns a unique library of works on hydropathy, and many interesting documents about Graefenberg during his father-in-law's life-time.

I have to thank Mrs. Hughan, of Hughan Castle, Graefenberg, for her hospitality and courtesy during my visit ; and Miss M. Behr for her translations of books and MSS. from the German.

R. METCALFE.

Priessnitz House,
    Richmond Hill,
        Surrey.

CONTENTS

LIST OF ILLUSTRATIONS

LIST OF ILLUSTRATIONS

VINCENT PRIESSNITZ

—•◦•—

INTRODUCTION

WATER applications have been used and appreciated throughout the ages. Vincent Priessnitz — who earned the title " Father of Hydropathy "—was neither the discoverer of, nor the first to use, water as a remedial agent in disease.

That discovery was probably coeval with the appearance of man in his present condition. When we see that some of the lower animals possess an instinctive knowledge that water is good for them when wounded, and in certain conditions of sickness—for they have been seen to seek that element when they are suffering—we should be derogating from man's dignity and superior intellectual endowments if we denied to him a similar instinct and equal observing powers.

Histories that carry us back to remote ages

show that the practice of water ablution, both for sanitary and religious purposes, existed amongst most ancient peoples.

Among the Jews bathing was enjoined by a code of specific regulations, which served to secure personal cleanliness and to convey the idea of moral purity. The association of water with the cure of disease is illustrated by Elisha's command to Naaman the Syrian to wash seven times in Jordan ; by that of the Saviour to the blind man to go and wash in the pool of Siloam ; and by the resort of the sick to the pool of Bethesda. Among the Egyptians, Greeks and Romans, baths were in common use. Most of us have heard of the Greek gymnasia and the Roman thermæ, in which the plunge or affusion was largely employed as an invigorator of the body.

Mahomet enjoined the use of the bath, and wherever his followers are it is in daily use. In almost all countries, hot or cold, civilized or savage, some form of bathing has been and is practised. Its utility for purposes of health, cleanliness and comfort is practically acknowledged everywhere.

The fathers of the healing art, whose names have become familiar to us, were well aware of the therapeutic virtues of water. Pythagoras (B.C. 530), and somewhat later Hippocrates (B.C. 460), used water, with friction and rubbing, in spasms and diseases of the joints, and watery applications in a great variety of diseases—particularly pneumonia, gout and rheumatism. The successors of these sages, up to the time of Galen (A.D. 131-200), valued water in the treatment of disease. Galen himself gave water the highest place in his list of remedies. "Cold water," he says, "quickens the action of the bowels, provided there be no constriction from spasms, when warm is to be used; cold drinks stop hæmorrhages and sometimes bring back heat; cold drinks are good in continued and ardent fevers. They discharge the peccant and redundant humours by stool, or by vomiting, or by sweat." He recommends tepid and warm water drinking, with hot baths, followed by tepid or cold, in cases of biliousness, spasms, fever of the stomach, hiccup, cholera morbus, obstinate ophthalmia and plethora.

Not much is recorded of the use of water in disease after Galen's time until the Arabian physicians Rhazes (923) and Avicenna (1036) are found advocating the use of cold water in fevers, measles, small-pox, vomiting, nausea and diarrhœa. About this time the Arabs were prosecuting their researches in chemistry and pharmacy; many new drugs were introduced and water was ignored, and, judging from the results of the Arabian treatment of disease, not to the advantage of the patients.

Here and there, in the medical history of Europe, there occurs the name of a doctor who recommends water-drinking, washing, bathing, or swimming, to preserve health and cure disease. But there is nothing of special importance until the beginning of the eighteenth century (1702), when our countrymen, Sir John Floyer and Dr. Baynard, published their "ΨΥΧΡΟΛΟΤΣΙ'Α : or the History of Cold Bathing, both Ancient and Modern," the first part of which contains interesting letters by Floyer, written between the years 1696 and 1702. In Italian, at Naples (1723), appeared Lanzani's " Right Method of Using Cold Water in Fever and Other Maladies, Internal and External."

Niccolo Lanzani mostly confines his advocacy of water to its employment internally in fevers of all kinds, for which he holds water-drinking to be the best remedy.

About the same time appeared another interesting book by a distinguished clergyman, John Hancocke, D.D., Rector of St. Margaret's, Lothbury, London, Prebendary of Canterbury, entitled, " Febrifugum Magnum, or Common Water the Best Cure for Fevers and probably for the Plague" (1722), in which he gives many instances of the curative effects of water, used in cases of fever, violent colds, etc., unassisted by any kind of medicine. These publications, with the actual practice of the authors, again drew attention to water as a remedial agent. Floyer and Baynard employed water freely and with success in chronic diseases, such as rheumatism, gout, paralysis, indigestion, general debility and nervous affections. Externally, they administered the plunge bath, and they gave copious doses of water internally.

About this time several pamphlets about water treatment appeared. Amongst them was the following:

"The Curiosities of Common Water; or, the Advantages thereof in Preventing and Curing Many Distempers, etc." By John Smith. (London: 1723.)

Thomas Taylor, the "Water Poet," is responsible for a pamphlet with the following title: "Kick for kick and Cuff for cuff, a clear stage and no favour; or, a refutation of a bombastical, scurrilous postscript, wrote by one who calls himself Gabriel John, others still will have it Daniel Defoe, which he calls reflections on my Hudibrastick reply to his Flagellum or dry answer to Dr. Hancocke's liquid book, etc. With two remarkable instances of cures by common water, one of a malignant fever and no less than seven in one family of the pestilence." Published in London, 1723.

In German there appeared a book, "On the Power and Effect of Cold Water" (1738), by

J. S. Hahn, who lived in the neighbourhood of Graefenberg, and whose father, Dr. S. Hahn, was a worshipper of cold water. This Hahn, though he used other remedies, employed water so extensively in curing diseases that he may be considered a sort of hydropathist. He recommends cold water in chronic diseases particularly; also *washing* in small-pox and eruptions of the skin, *falling baths* in inflammation of the brain, *douches* in maimings, *cold injections* in diarrhœa, *injections* into the *nostrils* for colds, and *into the ears* for deafness, and *footbaths* in chronic injuries. Hahn's work had, in 1754, passed through four editions. It did not, however, succeed in winning over the faculty to the cause of the water-cure; and as for the public of Germany, though they liked to drink water, they did not care to have it applied externally.

V. Perez, a Spanish physician, sought to cure most diseases by the use of water, and he published at Madrid, in 1753, a small 4to. book entitled, " El Promotor de la Salud de los Hombres, sin dispendio el menor de sus caudales; admirable methodo de curar todo mal con brevedad, sequridad, y à placer. Dissertacion histórico, crítico, médico, prática, en que se establece el aqua por remedio universal de las dolencias."

Somewhat later, in England, Fred. Hoffman published his ideas (London, 1761) with a somewhat similar title: "An Essay on the Nature and Properties of Water, showing its prodigious use; and proving it to be an universal medecine, both for preventing and curing the diseases to which the human body is subject."

About 1777, an English doctor—Wright—was led to try the water-cure. Dr. Wright, having caught fever from a sailor, undressed, threw a cloak about him, and went on deck, where, doffing his cloak, he had three pails of water thrown over his head. Repeating the process as often as the feverish heat returned, he quite recovered. Afterwards he treated fevers successfully in Edinburgh by the cold affusion, and published a report of his proceedings in the *London Medical Journal* (1786). By the same method Dr. Currie, of Liverpool, (1750-1805) treated with great success a contagious fever which was prevalent in that town, and in 1797 made public his views and experiences, with a list of cures effected by his measures. Though he by no means anticipated the discoveries of the founder of hydropathy, his reports on the effects of water in fevers and other diseases are considered to possess much practical value.

Dr. Currie found imitators both in England and on the Continent, to whose names and achievements it would be tedious to refer. But in connection with the therapeutic use of water it would be unpardonable to omit mention of the name of the great German physician, Hufeland, who may be regarded as an apostle of bathing. After Hufeland, and before Priessnitz, by far the greatest water-doctor was Professor Oertel, of Ansbach, whose numerous writings on the subject became quite popular. Oertel's motto, "Drink water in abundance, the more the better; for it prevents and cures all evils," found a large measure of acceptance with the people of the Continent. Water societies were formed in Germany, and water was extensively used dietetically and medicinally, with, as was supposed, admirable effect. Still, there was no system, and what was done was done very much at random.

It remained for one greater and more far-sighted to grasp at once the whole secret of water treatment, and to develop and systematize it in one short life-time.

That man was Vincent Priessnitz.

CHAPTER I

IN Austrian Silesia, at the foot of the southern mountains of Moravia, called the Sudetes, is the prettily situated town of Freiwaldau, watered by the two small rivers Biela and Scharitz.

Freiwaldau can be traced as far back as the thirteenth century. It is said to derive its name from *Frei* (open) and *Waldau* (space in a forest). It has nearly six thousand inhabitants, mostly weavers, and contains a celebrated linen manufactory. From Freiwaldau a road ascends to a mountain called the Graefenberg—" the pearl of the Sudetes "—one of the promontories of the Hirschbad Kamm (Stag's Bath Ridge), which forms part of the range of the Sudetes. The Graefenberg rises to two thousand feet above the level of the Baltic Sea.

There, towards the middle of last century, several inhabitants of Freiwaldau settled on their properties, and whilst retaining their rights as citizens

9

of Freiwaldau, formed a colony of their own. This was the origin of a new hamlet, which took its name of Graefenberg from the mountain on which it was founded.

In this hamlet of Graefenberg was born, at the end of last century, a boy who was to become of the greatest importance to humanity.

Vincent Priessnitz saw the light of day on October 4, 1799, at Graefenberg, and was christened on the following day at the parish church of Freiwaldau. His ancestors had lived for centuries in that neighbourhood. The name of Priessnitz occurs in old chronicles, and lives in the legendary lore of Austrian Silesia. The spring in the woods of the Hirschkamm, called the Priessnitz Spring, has been known under that name for two centuries. One of Vincent Priessnitz's ancestors was killed there by Swedish soldiers in the Thirty Years' War. During his absence they had invaded his house and carried away his lovely daughter. He pursued, overtook them at the above-named spring, and in the endeavour to free his beloved child, lost his life in a most cruel manner.

Vincent Priessnitz was the youngest of five children. His father, one of the small farmers at Graefenberg, was known as an able and experienced man in his calling. His mother, a daughter of a smith at Lindewiese, enjoyed the reputation of a hard‑working, capable, and God‑fearing woman. She was, in a high degree, order‑loving, and enforced good principles on her children and servants, whom she expected to begin their day's work at four o'clock in the morning.

In order to learn reading and writing and the rudiments of arithmetic, Vincent was sent to school at Freiwaldau. Regular attendance at school did not last long, for scarcely had he completed his sixth year when his elder brother, who was to have taken over the farm work, died of brain‑fever in 1805. This sad event so grieved his father that his eyes, which for some time had been in a weak state, rapidly grew worse, and he became totally blind, shortly after Vincent had completed his eighth year, in 1807. His mother now made the boy work much on the farm, so that young Priessnitz could but seldom attend school. Nevertheless, he became proficient in reading and arithmetic, whereas in writing, which requires a good deal of application, he remained backward. During his whole life it was a great exertion, and it required considerable self‑control on his part to wield a pen.

Already, at this early age, Priessnitz showed unusual abilities, especially an excellent memory, acute perception, and a remarkably vivid and happy power of observation. He lived a great deal out of doors, and early remarked the effect which changes of temperature had, not only on himself, but on plants and on the animals confided to his care. As he noted with accuracy manifestations of life in the animal world, it did not escape his observation that wounded or otherwise maimed animals plunged their injured limbs into cold water.

When resting beneath the shade of a tree, near his favourite Priessnitz-quelle, watching the herd confided to his care, he observed an incident which (he used to say) first turned his attention to the effects of cold water. Sitting day-dreaming there, his attention was attracted by seeing a young roe, which had been shot through the thigh, drag itself with difficulty to the source of the spring. Then he saw how it managed to get its wounded thigh in such a position as to have it entirely covered with the flowing water. Priessnitz, with breathless interest, scarcely daring to move, watched the poor creature. He saw it return at short intervals to renew the bath during the day; it probably did so also during the night. Great was his joy to observe the animal improve from day to day, till it finally got well.

In his leisure hours, of which he had not many, the boy Vincent was fond of roaming in the neighbourhood not far from his father's property. Many times he may have quenched his thirst with a draught of the pure, delicious water from the spring, and it is not unlikely that even then he realized how life-giving and refreshing the water from this clear mountain-spring was; if tired, he rested by the pleasant waters, and listened to the sounds which spoke to him in a language at once familiar and yet mysterious. There it was that the fancy came of an unseen being, whispering into his ears words whose meaning he could not understand. And strange, unfamiliar feelings filled the lad's heart, and his spirit seemed to soar away and above the ordinary surroundings, to dwell in the magic land of dreams and aspirations.

In the Silesian valley lived several men of the people who enjoyed a certain reputation for having effected successful cures. One of them treated different diseases with herbs; another set fractured legs, another broken ribs. Especially clever in the manipulation of fractured legs and ribs was Ignatz Weisser, who lived over against the mill in the village of Sandhuebel; he was well known for many miles round, and was much sought after. It happened that on winter evenings the conversation in old Priessnitz's parlour sometimes turned on the cures effected by these men, while Vincent in a dark corner of the room listened. The vague ideas which had passed through his mind on those occasions were destined ere long to take shape, and to become illumined by a vivid light.

With young Priessnitz's natural tendency and

special disposition for practical observation, it was to be foreseen that these vague aspirations would give way by degrees to definite practical aims. He had from an early age been occupied with agricultural pursuits, and his clear and penetrating mind found ample opportunity for observations of varied kinds. Thus he noticed that domestic animals, and those employed for farming purposes, soon recovered from their ailments when treated with cold water. After repeated experiments on injuries resulting from various causes, he resolved to try the effect of cold-water applications on himself. This met with the happiest results. In consequence, he began to advise others to use cold water for the cure of bruises or other hurts, and thus became, at the age of fifteen (1814), a kind of medical adviser to his neighbours. Priessnitz worked his father's farm with circumspection and activity. Nearly the whole of the outside management lay on his youthful shoulders, as his blind father was unable to render much assistance. His life was more than once endangered while accomplishing some arduous task. On one occasion he had driven into the forest on his sledge to bring it home laden with wood, and was guiding the horse to re-enter the yard, when he slipped, and the heavily loaded sledge went over part of his body. Owing to the fortunate presence of a labourer, who, seeing the coming danger, gave the sledge a vigorous push, the youth's life was saved, and he escaped without serious injury.

Another time he was driving a sledge loaded with heavy beams. The road was slippery, and he was driving fast. Suddenly the sledge struck against a rock with such force that the heavy iron axe which was lying on the sledge was sent flying past the driver's face, almost grazing it. On a third occasion Priessnitz was not so fortunate. It was in 1816, when he was in his eighteenth year; he was driving a large van loaded with oats, destined for a neighbouring field. On its way the horse shied, frightened by some trifling cause, and took the bit between his teeth. Priessnitz tried to prevent his running away, when the horse struck out so violently with his hind legs that Priessnitz was thrown, and had his front teeth knocked out, the heavy waggon passing right over his body. The lad became unconscious, and remained so until the surgeon arrived from Freiwaldau, who pronounced his life in immediate danger, adding that in the most favourable case he would remain an invalid for life, unfit for any hard work. This depressing verdict was a terrible blow to Priessnitz. He who filled the blind father's place, on whom rested the responsibility of working the farm —he was never to get well again. In this terrible plight he had compresses made of herbs, stewed in wine, according to the doctor's prescription. However, instead of getting relief from the excruciating pains, they increased, and became unbearable; so at last he tore the hot compress off, throwing it aside in despair. Then he remembered how the miller from Sandhuebel used to dress broken ribs. Priessnitz had an oaken armchair brought, and proceeded to place his abdomen on the edge of it, holding his breath and pressing the abdomen upwards, until the broken ribs got back (as he thought) into their natural position. He had cold bandages fixed across the chest; the acute pains diminished, and he fell into a deep sleep. He continued these compresses of linen towels, steeped in cold water, well wrung out, changing the bandages at intervals, and drinking a good deal of cold water, which prevented feverish symptoms being set up, as is usual in fractures of this kind. After several days, he was so far recovered as to be able to superintend his work at the farm.*

* "Letters from Gräfenberg," by John Gibbs, 1847. Priessnitz related to Captain Claridge: "Having broken two of my ribs, and a surgeon having told me that I never could be cured so as to be fit for work again, I resolved to endeavour to cure myself. My first care was to replace my ribs, and this I did by leaning with my abdomen with all my might against a chair, and holding my breath so as to swell out my chest. The painful operation was attended with the success I expected. The ribs being replaced, I applied wet bandages to the part affected, drank plentifully of water, ate sparingly, and remained in perfect repose. In ten days I was able to get out."

Priessnitz wore the wet compress for a year, when he considered himself cured, and the only trace the injuries left was a slight depression on the left side of the chest, over the region of the heart. While his quick recovery was due to the constant application of wet bandages, yet there is no doubt that some of the vital organs received a permanent injury.

As an evidence of this, Priessnitz, after his accident, never enjoyed such robust health as before.

At the commencement of this century surgery was at a low ebb, as compared with the present day, and it would appear that Priessnitz's ribs were not properly set and bandaged. I was given to understand by his relatives that Priessnitz had a strong piece of towelling sewn on tightly to keep the ribs in position; this was never removed till the pain had ceased; he wore a wet bandage over it, re-wetted when dry. Notwithstanding Priessnitz's and the surgeon's efforts, the post-mortem examination showed that the broken ribs had not been properly set; and it is fairly certain that had Priessnitz carried out the surgeon's advice he would have died from the injuries.

The mere fact of telling this youth of eighteen that he would be an invalid all his life roused him in self-defence to try what wet bandages and water-drinking would do in his case, and the results

17   C

obtained fully justified the means employed. It is fair to conclude that if the broken ribs had been efficiently set, Priessnitz might have been spared a great deal of suffering, and have lived long enough to see his system established in every hospital, to the benefit of surgery and humanity at large.

CHAPTER II

His Life : 1817—1844

PRIESSNITZ'S faith in the healing power of cold water now became established. If he heard of anyone having bruises, dislocations, sprained limbs, or any other external injuries, he lost no time in recommending cold water as the means of obtaining a thorough and speedy cure; and in many cases he applied it himself.

As Priessnitz was generally fortunate in his treatment, his reputation soon spread beyond his own district, so that he was invited to Bohemia and Moravia before he had completed his nineteenth year (1818). At that time he only used a sponge for giving his ablutional treatment. The youthful appearance of the doctor, the many cures obtained by such simple means, made Priessnitz appear in the light of a sorcerer in the eyes of the peasant population.

As long as he gave his advice and cured people

gratis, he was looked upon by his neighbours as a benefactor.

But when strangers came to seek advice and help from this young water-doctor, and in return gave substantial proofs of their gratitude, the language of his former admirers underwent a marked change. Many a one who came to Graefenberg to ask where the water-doctor lived had for answer: "To the water-doctor you want to go? Why take the trouble to go to see that man? He is nothing but a quack!"

Envy and persecution were soon no longer confined to the peasant population of the villages. Medical men from Freiwaldau and the neighbourhood began to notice the young man, and became aware of a rival who considerably reduced the number of their patients. With the help of the local authorities they contrived to put constant difficulties and annoyances in his way.

Many of those whom Priessnitz had cured had now to appear before the magistrates, where they were questioned as to the nature of their complaints, and as to the method employed by Priessnitz in curing them. This was done in order to bring accusations against them. Amongst these men was a miller named Franz Nietsche, whom the doctors had given up, and who had been completely restored to health by Priessnitz from a severe and tedious illness. The magistrate cross-questioned the miller, and he was ordered to say *who* had cured him, it being known that he had been treated by the doctors as well as by Priessnitz. The man, who looked well and hearty, replied: " They all have helped me—the doctors, the apothecaries, and Priessnitz. The two former helped me to get rid of my money, and Priessnitz to get rid of my illness."

Amongst others, several priests accused the false prophet, as they called him, and without investigation into Priessnitz's proceedings, warned the people against " the new superstition."

The curate of Vogelseifen, in Silesia, was exceedingly wroth when he heard of the Graefenberg farmer's water-cures, and threatened to have him imprisoned if ever he showed himself in church amongst the congregation.

Yet shortly after this same pastor had cause to alter his opinion entirely, both of the water-cure and its inventor. The reverend gentleman had been suffering for years from a chronic affection which had baffled the skill of his doctors. Finally a serious throat disease declared itself, together with an affection of the liver. This brought him so low that he was unable to take the journey to some baths which the doctors had ordered for him. In this plight he sent for Priessnitz, and asked the much-abused water-doctor to help him.

The young man's calm and dignified demeanour made a favourable impression upon the priest, and he placed himself entirely in the hands of " the false prophet."

Priessnitz began to treat the reverend gentleman without delay, and was so successful that his patient was able to preach again after only a fortnight's treatment.

Thus his former enemy became his warm and sincere friend.

He now advised Priessnitz to study thoroughly his profession, and placed books on medicine at his disposal. Priessnitz took a few of them home, and after an attentive perusal, returned them, remarking that nothing he had read therein led him to alter his own opinion, declining at the same time to read any more books on the subject, as he was afraid, so he expressed himself, that they might warp his mind.

The pastor agreed with him, and became henceforth a zealous follower of the water-cure, and from the same pulpit whence he had previously attacked so fiercely and accused so unjustly the innocent man, he owned his error, asking Priessnitz's forgiveness before the whole assembly.

It has been asserted by an eminent authority on hygienic medicine that Priessnitz owed his wonderful experience to his ignorance of medical science. This ignorance was to his great advantage, for what does the history of medicine offer but a discouraging picture of the instability of principles, a series of theories succeeding each other without any one of them being able to content an upright spirit, or satisfy an inquiring mind?

Without wishing to infer that medical training is not an advantage, it is pretty clear that in Priessnitz's case it was unnecessary, and it is fair to conclude that, but for such laymen, the public would never have heard of hydropathy from our recognised schools of medicine.

About the year 1822 the old wooden house where his parents and himself had lived was pulled down, and replaced by a stone building.

Priessnitz's time was much taken up with attending persons who had purposely come to Graefenberg to be cured by his treatment. The ever-increasing number of strangers coming from all parts for the cure made it necessary to build houses to receive them. Priessnitz tried, as much as lay in his power, to meet this want, and had a large stone building erected, as well as several smaller wooden ones.

During his mother's lifetime Priessnitz had her invaluable aid in the management of the household, but unfortunately he lost his good mother in 1826. She died from an accident, having been tossed by a bull.

The difficulties which arose for Priessnitz in the household management after his mother's death were, however, not of long duration. The same clear judgment, the same art, which brought blessings on so many, and which had already brought him fame and worldly goods, was also destined to lay the foundation of his domestic happiness.

In the neighbouring village of Boehmischdorf, the wife of the much respected and wealthy magistrate had for many years suffered from gout. Doctors and chemists had long tried in vain to alleviate the unhappy woman's sufferings. As nobody was able to do anything for her, she consented at last, although reluctantly, to consult Priessnitz. In this way he was enabled to see their charming daughter, for whom he felt a sincere and growing attachment. His modest and manly ways won him the daughter's heart, while his successful treatment made him the friend of the parents.

February 5, 1828, was the happy, long-looked-for day on which the beloved Sophie became his wife, and thus was brought about the fulfilment of the dearest wish of his heart.

Priessnitz had not been mistaken in his choice, for by the side of his excellent wife he found a haven of rest from the storms of adverse circumstances which from time to time burst over

SOFIE PRIESSNITZ.

(ABOUT 1830.)

To face p. 24.

his head during his much - agitated career. A
rare treasure was this amiable and superior
woman. To a temperament at once natural and
gay was joined the gentleness of disposition of
a Christian spirit, whilst she showed herself full
of judgment and foresight in the management of
her large and complicated household.

Priessnitz's acute observation and growing experience made him more and more successful in
the exercise of his art. Not only was there a
rapid increase in the number of strangers seeking
relief at Graefenberg, but many were the calls
to visit patients in different parts of the country
who were unable to leave their homes. As far
as lay in his power he responded to these calls,
and thereby frequently encountered dangers likely
to cause the loss of limb and life.

He had been visiting a patient at Altstadt in
Moravia. The season was far advanced, the
morning raw and cold, as he mounted his horse
to start on his journey home. The road lay
across a bridge made slippery by the early frost.
He had scarcely gone half-way over when his
horse slipped, rolled over, and threw its rider
into the depths below. Priessnitz, to his astonish-
ment, found himself standing on his feet, and saw
how his horse had rolled over again, and then also
got on to its feet. He picked up his hat, which
he found lying close by, scaled the height to the

bridge, mounted his horse, and continued his journey.

By reason of his great success and the original method of his cures, he became the object of antagonism and of repeated attacks by members of the medical profession whom he had superseded.

In the year 1829, at which period began the printing of yearly lists of the visitors at Graefenberg, an accusation was brought against Priessnitz, charging him with being a quack doctor, who, in opposition to the laws of the country, undertook to treat patients without being authorized to practise by proper license from a faculty or other Government authority.

The Freiwaldau magistrate sentenced the accused to several days' imprisonment, with the additional punishment of fasting.

The appeal Priessnitz made to the higher court was followed by suspension of the verdict, and as, in the meanwhile, satisfactory reports relative to his character and medical treatment had arrived from the highest quarters, he obtained in the year 1831 an official permission to conduct a hydropathic establishment.

This establishment was only to be used for cleansing purposes, and only visitors residing in the neighbourhood were to be received.

However, patients whom the doctors had given up, and who had come from distant parts with

VINCENT PRIESSNITZ.

(ABOUT 1830.)

To face p. 26.

letters of recommendation, were not easily to be got rid of. And such sufferers arrived in increasing numbers, especially after the publication of a pamphlet by Dr. A. H. Kroeber, of Breslau, which loudly proclaimed the reputation of this Silesian restorer of health.*

Renewed complaints from the doctors, and inquiries on the part of the Government of one of the German States, determined the Imperial Home Office in Vienna to send one of its officials, Baron Turkheim, to Graefenberg, with the commission to investigate personally the state of affairs on the spot.

Court Councillor Turkheim, a man of scientific education, high culture, as well as a State official, was decidedly a proper person to undertake a mission of such far-reaching importance, and to judge of the actual state of affairs with impartiality.

Upon his arrival at Freiwaldau, during the summer of 1838, Baron Turkheim was welcomed by several ladies belonging to Vienna society, and they, together with a number of gentlemen occupying high positions in the Empire, gave him a satisfactory report about Priessnitz and his method

* " Priessnitz in Graefenberg, and his Method of using Cold Water in the Various Diseases of the Human Body," by Dr. A. H. Kroeber. Published by Joseph Max and Co., Breslau, 1833. In the German language.

of healing. He verified all he had heard as he became personally acquainted with Priessnitz, and ascertained beyond doubt that nobody was less of a quack or an impostor. He observed that, professionally, Priessnitz strictly adhered to the simple laws of health, and used cold water in various ways as his sole healing agent, to the exclusion of all so-called medicines; at the same time either making use of his own unique experience, based upon observation, or following the inspirations of his genius.

Baron Turkheim made on Priessnitz and his establishment a favourable report. We give a few extracts from this report on the Silesian " Naturarzt " (physician of Nature), which shows that the writer was a man of noble character and sound judgment. His conduct in this matter will cause his name ever to be honourably associated with that of Priessnitz.*

" That Priessnitz is no ordinary man even his enemies must admit. He is no impostor, but is filled with the purest zeal to help others whenever he is able to do so; and he is particularly fitted to do this. The number of those who call Priessnitz

* James Wilson, M.D., "The Water Cure," 1842. Baron Turkheim, being at a medical society in Vienna, was asked what he thought of the new charlatanism; he replied : " Priessnitz is no impostor, he beats us in his prognosis, and is more successful in his practice. Believe me, you have much to learn from this 'countryman.' "

GRAEFENBERG.

(1839.)

To face p. 28.

a quack, and a man of selfish motives, only constitute a small minority, and are mostly doctors and
surgeons from the surrounding districts whose
incomes are reduced by his practice, and who
therefore get up complaints against him.

" Unassuming, modest, ever ready to give his
patients help, untiring by day and night, obliging,
firm and consistent in his actions, Priessnitz possesses qualities which are inadmissible in an
impostor. Notwithstanding the most careful in-
vestigations, I have been unable to trace a single
instance wherein he was actuated by selfish
motives. Whether his establishment has imper-
fections, whether he has restored to health many
or only a few, whether the complaints which he
has pronounced cured have returned after a longer
or shorter period, it remains certain that his
method of treatment in its details will always
continue to be one of great importance in the
domain of the art of healing. This new cure and
this extraordinary man, therefore, deserve the full
attention of the Government; moreover, any
serious interference would be entirely misplaced."

On the question whether the establishment at
Graefenberg should be allowed to go on, or whether
it ought to be closed, Baron Turkheim reported:

" The Imperial Commission has pronounced
unanimously against closing the Graefenberg
establishment, as it has proved itself efficient in

many cases, as no ill after-effects could be traced, and as the few cases of death are not sufficient reason for so doing, seeing that such cases occur constantly elsewhere and under the care of ordinary practitioners. To close this establishment would have a bad moral effect on the minds of the public, who have become familiarized with the great reputation it has won both at home and abroad. This is a point which deserves full consideration. Finally, it is both difficult and unadvisable to prohibit new treatments, and such a course of action might possibly have a demoralizing effect on the Austrian people.

"I, for my part, fully share this opinion, and admit all the motives brought forth by the Commission against closing the Graefenberg establishment."

This report, as made by Baron Turkheim to the Imperial Cabinet at Vienna, had beneficial results, both for Priessnitz and for adherents to the water-cure.

An order was issued in 1838 to the effect that Vincent Priessnitz was to enjoy the same privileges as members of the medical faculty in regard to the practice of hygienic remedies. In other words, a license to practise was granted to him by the sovereign of his own country, an honour that has not been granted to anybody since the foundation of our medical colleges.

From that time Priessnitz had to suffer, it is true, occasionally from private annoyances, but never again was he subjected to those public attacks by medical men which had formerly embittered his life. He was henceforth free to exercise his method of curing without interference, and gained daily new friends and admirers amongst all nations.

CHAPTER III

His Life: 1845

IN the autumn of 1845, Freiwaldau and Graefenberg were visited by his Imperial Highness
the Archduke Franz Karl. This patron and
promoter of institutions dedicated to the welfare
of mankind arrived at Graefenberg on September 27. He received there with great amiability a
deputation from the visitors, and accepted an
address presented to him by the deputation.

The members of this deputation were :

Don T. M. Gutierez Estrada, ex-Minister of
Foreign Affairs in Mexico ;

Count Czaski, Field-Marshal in Poland ;

Count Schaffgotsch, Gentleman-in-Waiting of
the Royal Prussian Court ;

Baron Sotzbeck, Gentleman-in-Waiting of the
Court of Bavaria ;

G. H. O. Moor, Captain of the 35th Regiment
of the Line ;

T. La Moile, French ex-Consul in Ireland.

The address was in French, and ran thus:

" We, the undersigned, born in different countries, and who at present are enjoying the hospitality and protection of a kindly Government,
joyfully seize the opportunity of your Highness's
presence here to offer to your Highness our most
respectful homage.

" We cannot refrain from giving expression to
the feeling of deep gratitude which animates all
present, for the grace accorded by your Highness's
exalted house to a method of healing which has
brought blessings on all here present, as well as
those absent ones who at different times have
returned with health renewed to their native countries. The establishments of Graefenberg and
Freiwaldau have enjoyed for a considerable time
the protection of a paternal Government, and
your Imperial Highness has not deemed them
unworthy of a personal visit to witness the efficacy
of a treatment which is spreading daily, and thus
saving the human race from the double curse of
intemperance and premature decay.

" At all times, and in all parts of the world, cold
water has been tried as a remedy, and as such has
been approved by eminent physicians. The inhabitants of Europe in the olden time made occa-
sional attempts to pierce the darkness of prejudice
and unscrupulousness, by making use of the

neglected but marvellous power of this gift of Nature.

" But these attempts were few, and at long intervals, thus only affording transitory glimpses of light.

" To Austria is destined the honour of calling her own the immortal discoverer of a new and efficient method of healing.

" A farmer, born in an obscure hamlet—Priessnitz—obeying the calls of his genius, like all great men, was able to overcome all difficulties, and to mount rapidly the path to fame and distinction. His keen and inquiring mind pierced the hidden secrets of Nature. By untiring observation and by experience only he brought to light facts which the science of centuries had been unable to discover.

" His marvellous cures were known at first only in the neighbouring districts, but by degrees his ever-increasing reputation spread to all parts of the world, shedding a brilliant light on the name of Priessnitz. Sufferers from every country came to submit, so to say, blindly to his treatment.

" Even a large number of the disciples of Æsculapius renounced their old prejudices to drink wisdom at the new spring of science; thus has the rustic cottage of Priessnitz become the refuge of suffering mankind, and his simple dwelling the cradle of a new creed.

"Far from being intoxicated by his great success and unexpected fortune, Priessnitz remained true to his simple habits, and never altered his mode of life. His only ambition was the accomplishment of his great work, and we do not know whether to admire more his rare genius, his perseverance, or his modesty.

"Full of admiration for the cold-water treatment and of gratitude to its illustrious inventor, we do not hesitate respectfully to offer this address to your Royal and Imperial Highness, as we have no doubt that your Highness's visit will be of great importance towards furthering the development and propagation of this beneficent treatment, the blessings of which have been felt by all here present."

* * * * *

In the evening a ball was given at Graefenberg, which was attended by his Imperial Highness. Amongst the guests of distinction were the Duchess of Anhalt-Koethen and the Prince-Bishop of Breslau, Baron of Diepenbrook.

On the following day the Archduke Franz Karl visited the Graefenberg establishments and inspected the douches, baths, etc.

He entered the large dining-hall while the patients were at breakfast, showed great interest in the arrangements, and took his leave amid the enthusiastic cheers of all present.

Priessnitz, who had explained the use of the different appliances, and answered the Archduke's questions on various matters in his accustomed quiet and dignified manner, received repeated marks of encouragement and approval from his august visitor.

Besides the Archduke Franz Karl, several other princes visited Graefenberg, including the King of Saxony, who desired to become acquainted with the extraordinary man who had been the means of displaying one of Nature's most precious secrets.

People suffering from serious and distressing diseases came from all parts of the world to this modern Delphi, to regain, if not always health, at least alleviation from their sufferings, under the directions and salutary influence of its high-priest.

At times Graefenberg presented a strange and interesting spectacle as the gathering-place of many nationalities.

These unusual doings in and near Graefenberg, especially the Archduke Franz Karl's visit, drew the higher authorities' attention to Priessnitz's sphere of action, but this time with a very different result to that on previous occasions. People suddenly remembered the excellent services this man had rendered during the cholera epidemic which some years previously had decimated Graefenberg and the neighbourhood, while not one fatal case was recorded amongst those who had been treated by Priessnitz. There could no longer exist any doubt as to the efficacy of the cold-water cure, and that Priessnitz, as the inventor of a new system, deserved to be ranked amongst the benefactors of suffering humanity.

It was often remarked that his private and public life, his family and social relations, were animated by a modest, manly, and Christian spirit.

Priessnitz's beneficent influence was not only felt by those who came to seek renewed health and strength under his care : the poorer population of Graefenberg and the surrounding districts owed to him the great improvement which by degrees took place in their circumstances.

In his earlier years, when the boy Priessnitz looked on the fields and homesteads of his native village, and those of the neighbouring districts, his eye met no cheering picture. The fields were stony, and only here and there a poor crop covered them sparingly. Emaciated cows tried almost in vain to feed on the neglected meadows. In the garden plots scarcely a fruit-tree was to be seen, and the cottages insufficiently sheltered a hungry population.

Very different was the scene on which he looked in later years from the so-called " Haeuschen." Rich cornfields dotted the landscape, herds of cattle were browsing on well-drained meadows ; gardens, gay with flowers, and orchards filled with fruit-laden trees, spoke of thrift and well-being, and men and women could be seen working with cheerful and happy faces. In place of the cottages had risen dwellings of stone. Agriculture had been improved in all its branches; industry and trade were enlarged; and all this was owing to the influence of one man.

The great and undeniable services which Priessnitz had rendered to the State and to humanity were now proclaimed by his admirers and patrons in high places, and the just and benevolent Emperor Ferdinand presented him with the large gold medal for civil merit.*

In May, 1846, the Mayor of Troppau fastened this acknowledgment of distinction on Priessnitz's breast, in the Town Hall of Freiwaldau, before a large assembly. It was a day of general rejoicing and festivity. A *Te Deum* was sung in the parish church, and was attended by a large congregation. In the evening a brilliant ball at Graefenberg concluded the day's proceedings, and host and guests shared in the general happiness and satisfaction.

With all his rare gifts and qualities, with all the numerous distinctions lavished upon him, and the fame which made his name known all over the civilized world, Priessnitz remained modest and unassuming to a rare degree. Not even

* The highest mark of distinction in Austria, awarded to only a very limited number of recipients.

a letter addressed to "Vincent Priessnitz, in Europe," which reached him from South America, affected him.

Priessnitz's personal appearance was that of a man of simple, and yet strong and powerful, character. His whole demeanour bore the stamp of energy; the expression of his face showed the thinker and the keen observer. He impressed one as a man who recognised the importance of his calling. This calling was evidently no other than that of a physician, which brought him a posthumous reputation, which will endure through all coming ages.

He dressed with simplicity. He generally wore a gray coat or a blouse, gray trousers, a light cap, and short boots. It was only on Sundays and high festivals that he assumed the dress of the inhabitants of towns. The mark of distinction received from his sovereign was reserved for gala-days, and nobody could persuade him to wear the smallest ribbon on ordinary occasions.

There were patients every year who took pleasure in seizing any opportunity to give some marks of affection and gratitude to their much-honoured physician. But if Priessnitz by chance heard anything of their intentions beforehand he always prevented the carrying out of their plans.

Such was the case on October 4 of the year 1846. The visitors wished to celebrate Priessnitz's birthday by some special festivities, for the kind and unselfish man objected to anything which entailed extra expense upon his patients.

Nevertheless, a few of his warmest friends and admirers resolved not to let the day pass without giving some expression to their feeling.

On his entering the great hall, he was greeted with loud acclamations and cheers. During a pause of the band towards the end of the dinner, a number of the members of the Freiwaldau Committee rose and asked the assembled company for a few minutes' attention. Instantly all conversation ceased, and Dr. Selinger, who occupied a seat at his host's side, got up, and after a few introductory words made the following speech :

"We live in a month rich with glorious memories. It is not my intention to point out their importance to those here assembled, but I cannot refrain from mentioning to-day, the fourth of October, which is of such high significance to us all. It is the day on which, years ago, the Almighty Creator presented the world with one of His chosen children. On that day He confided to that child a sacred mission, bidding him grow and prosper, and, when the time had come, to go out amongst his fellow-men, preaching to the suffering and weak ones the new Gospel of health. And so it came to pass, at the appointed time, the chosen man appeared like a ministering angel, healing the sick and suffering of his people. His wise counsel has become a staff for the weak ones to lean upon; his prompt and active help is like a sheet-anchor for the despairing ones, and his name is the symbol of healing and aiding for all those who stand in need of such.

"And this name—shall I tell it you? It is a name which has become known in every part of the world. It is as familiar on the distant shores of the Mississippi and Orinoco as on those of our own Rhine and Danube. The valleys of the Pyrenees have heard its sound, as well as the mountains of Scandinavia. It is the name of a man who has been deemed worthy of the greatest mark of distinction by his Imperial Master, the august sovereign of this country—a name which has found its place already in the book of contemporary history, but which future records will exalt yet more. We also have been attracted by it to this small village—small in size, but great in fame. Almost every nationality of the whole civilized world is represented here, and whatever differences may divide us, one common tie binds us together—the tie of deep and heartfelt gratitude; and so I may hope to find an echo in everyone's heart here present when I say: 'Long live Priessnitz!'"

Loud and ringing cheers interrupted the

speaker, and "Vivats" and enthusiastic cries in all languages filled the hall.

The large assembly now became much excited, and everyone pressed round their beloved physician to give expression to their feelings of gratitude and respect.

Priessnitz was visibly affected, embraced his friend, and thanked the assembly, but never again did he appear in the large hall at dinner on his birthday.

The following Sunday, October 11, was a day of great solemnity in Freiwaldau and the neighbouring districts.

His Grace the Prince-Bishop of Breslau was going to celebrate on that day the rite of Confirmation. A large number of the visitors at Graefenberg seized this opportunity to offer the venerable ecclesiastic a solemn welcome.

At the express wish of the Graefenberg colony, Dr. Selinger received the Bishop with an address. He said in this address that all nations had come to these parts to seek help and advice from the renowned physician Priessnitz; that they were constantly reminded when enjoying Nature among the lovely mountains and forests of the neighbourhood, or getting rest and refreshment at the numerous health-giving springs, that they were enjoying the hospitality of a high-minded and unprejudiced monarch, the promoter and patron of the water-cure. This feeling of gratitude had made them desirous of giving it expression on the present occasion of his Grace's presence at Freiwaldau.

The Bishop, a man of great culture, answered in an appropriate speech, expressing his appreciation of the visitors' feelings, and hoping that they would derive as much benefit from the water-cure as he himself had done nine years before. Finally, he looked round for Priessnitz, whom he at last discovered at a distance effacing himself in the crowd. The Prince beckoned to him to approach, and shook hands with him.

In church, before the beginning of the Confirmation, the Bishop, in a short address to the congregation, mentioned that he owed his health to the exertions of one of them, and that he was glad to be able to show his gratitude by the solemnization of the rite of Confirmation that day.

With all his modesty and simplicity, Priessnitz was quite aware of his high destination. His noble self-reliance protected him against all petty embarrassment and timidity, and enhanced his often-admired presence of mind, which never forsook him on any occasion.

A Prince of a reigning house one day admired the pretty and tasteful arrangement of banners and arms—presents of different patients—in the dining-hall at Graefenberg,* when a French abbé, otherwise neatly dressed, entered bare-headed and bare-footed. The Prince, who was conversing with Priessnitz, noticed this peculiar appearance, and smilingly asked his host :

"Are your patients in the habit of going about in this fashion ?"

"Yes, your Royal Highness," answered Priessnitz, "always, when they suffer from cold feet."

There is no doubt that Priessnitz had great reason to dislike the medical profession. He did not hate it, but neither did he love it. Medical men were not personally sympathetic to him, and, considering how different to his were their ideas on the preservation of the health of mankind, this antipathy can easily be understood. If one had seen how cruelly some of these gentlemen behaved towards this excellent man, how clumsy they often showed themselves in their professional capacity, one would not be surprised at the want of sympathy and confidence on his part.

There were some whose reputation had never travelled beyond the confines of their native village, and who gave themselves airs of such overbearing vanity in the presence of the celebrated

* Besides these beautifully worked and costly banners, about thirty in number, presented by patients of as many different nationalities, this hall is decorated now with fine life-size portraits of the Emperor Francis Joseph I. and Vincent Priessnitz.

To face p. 41.

DINING-HALL IN THE OLD CURHAUS.

physician, that only a Priessnitz could have re-
frained from giving vent to just anger.

Another would perhaps, when taking a walk
some fine morning with one of the patients under
treatment, condescend to inspect the douches and
springs of Graefenberg and the neighbourhood,
and would forthwith send into the world a pamphlet or an article to announce that he had been
initiated by Priessnitz himself into the practice of
the water-cure.

A third, under the mask of an admirer, would
try to get access to the master of Graefenberg,
afterwards only to deride and mock him behind
his back.

A fourth, who had been cured from some long-
standing and weary illness by the kind-hearted
Priessnitz, would get admission into the houses of
rich and influential people, pretending there to
serve his benefactor and propagate the water
treatment; instead of which, his object once
attained, he proclaimed the difficulties and drawbacks of the treatment, and promised to cure with
drugs long-standing sufferings in the shortest
space of time.

Priessnitz's worst pupils were medical men. It
is difficult for people to free themselves from an
acquired method and to start an entirely new
one.

"Doctors have learned too much," Priessnitz

used to say. "If they wish to become good water-doctors, they must begin by forgetting a great deal of their previous experience in the treatment of diseases by medicine. Doctors have neither knowledge of, nor faith in, the healing virtue of cold water, and therefore do not use it with the necessary confidence."

The knowledge of this filled Priessnitz with apprehension, and he often said sadly to his friends : " If, after my death, my establishment should fall into the hands of a doctor, it will soon be ruined."

CHAPTER IV

Closing Years: 1846—1848

THE years of 1846-47 were years of famine in the greater part of Europe.

This was a time of deep unhappiness for Priessnitz, whose loving heart bled to witness so much misery. If the number of sufferers was great, the number of those who looked on in idle selfishness was not less considerable. Instead of coming forward to relieve the unfortunate ones, who often were driven from place to place to seek food and shelter, men and women of means preferred to retire into their own comfortable houses, keeping their money safely under lock and key, while around them people were crying for help and dying of want and exposure. Priessnitz listened to this cry of distress, and came forward to give his help in a way which deserves not to be forgotten.

Between 100 and 200, and at the time of greatest need 300, people received food daily in

47

his house. Never a day passed without Priessnitz and his wife helping from forty to fifty persons in some way to tide over this terrible time. One may safely ascribe to their untiring exertions in the cause of the poor and needy the quiet and order which reigned throughout Graefenberg and the neighbouring districts during these critical years.

The year 1847 threatened to be a fatal one for Priessnitz. In consequence of the unusual heat of the preceding summer, frequent night-duty, arduous attendance on severe cases, and the pernicious habit of prescribing during mealtimes, Priessnitz felt weak, and suffered for some time.

The separation from his beloved daughter Sophie brought on a catastrophe. Sophie had been married on January 26, 1847, in the parish church of Freiwaldau, to a Hungarian nobleman, Joseph von Ujhazy, proprietor of the estate Budamir, near Kaschau.

On the following day the young couple took leave of their dear ones to go on their wedding tour. The parting from this deeply-loved child had a depressing effect on Priessnitz. The same day, after dinner, on leaving the large hall for his private apartments, he fell down unconscious in the corridor.

The news of the occurrence spread rapidly through the establishment. A panic seized the assembled visitors; they lost presence of mind, and it was thought advisable to send for a Danish doctor, who lived close by in the Graefenberg colony.

Meanwhile the insensible Priessnitz had been taken into his secretary's room. When the doctor arrived and wanted to see the patient, one of the visitors, Baron von R., peremptorily refused his admittance, declaring that in this establishment no other treatment but the water-cure should be made use of.

And so it happened that two students of the water-treatment were enabled to give evidence of their ability. One was Mr. Bochin, Priessnitz's secretary, the other a Mr. Matezki, a former patient; both had studied under Priessnitz for a considerable time.

After friction with the hands, wetted with water, and with the help of two bathing attendants, and some other appliances, they had the unspeakable satisfaction, after several hours' exertion, to see, towards midnight, their beloved master out of danger. After having recovered consciousness, Priessnitz was able to prescribe how to treat the scarlet fever which had now declared itself. These prescriptions were carried out so successfully that he was able to resume his work in less than a week, and to pay his accustomed visits to Frei-waldau, to the intense delight of his patients.

The general happiness at his speedy recovery was indescribable. A feeling of how irreparable the loss of their physician would be struck terror in his patients' hearts, and the thought of his death and its probable consequences filled the inhabitants with trouble and apprehension.

The thanksgiving service, held on this occasion at the Freiwaldau parish church, was therefore attended by a large and deeply-moved congregation.

In January, 1848, his wife left him for some time to pay a visit to her daughter Sophie in Hungary. Although Priessnitz had all his children, except his eldest daughter, with him, he missed his dearly-loved wife painfully. During the whole time of her unwonted absence from home Priessnitz was in a state of agitation and unrest, and could scarcely await her return. It seemed to him as if his guardian angel had forsaken him.

On Madame Priessnitz's journey home she narrowly escaped a terrible accident, that was averted by the courage and presence of mind of the postilion and conductor of the postchaise, which was coming down a slippery mountain road with great speed. Arriving at the foot of the mountain more dead than alive with fright, she had the unspeakable joy of finding her husband, who, with deepest emotion, folded her in his arms.

The sunny and peaceful days which Priessnitz

was allowed to enjoy now in the midst of his family were but few in number.

The spring of 1848, and with it the Revolution, was approaching. To the religious and patriotic Priessnitz this was a great blow, which altered the tenor of his whole being. He, who never cared much about politics, now spoke about them incessantly. With his strictly conservative opinions and principles, the opposition he encountered daily became to him the source of a constant and bitter annoyance. To this was added anxiety about his married daughter in Hungary, whom he had not seen for fifteen months, and from whom he had had no news for a considerable time. He became irritable and suspicious, and lost his sunny enjoyment of life, which he began to liken to a bad dream. The strong and robust man became weak and languid, and when, after the termination of the civil war in 1849, his daughter Sophie came to see her beloved parents, she found the dear father ailing and much aged.

The Imperial Lieutenant Field Marshal, Prince Edmund von Schwarzenberg, whose arm became paralyzed after an apoplectic stroke, had made a successful cure at Graefenberg. His Highness Prince Adolph von Schwarzenberg, in a visit to Graefenberg (brought about by the just-mentioned circumstance), had arranged that for the period of six months, from October 1, 1849, till the end of

March, 1850, six sick officers of the Imperial Austrian army should be treated gratis at Graefenberg.
For each one of those who left cured another was
to come to take his place.*

Priessnitz showed great kindness to these officers
and also took charge on his own account of *eleven*
sick soldiers, not only giving them advice and the
treatment gratis, but providing them with board
and lodging gratuitously.

The Minister of War wrote to Priessnitz a
flattering acknowledgment of his services, which
ran as follows :

"VIENNA,
"*April* 28, 1850.

"The report of the inspectors of the establishment at Graefenberg certifies to the good effects
of your generous treatment of the six officers of
the Imperial Austrian Army who took the cold-
water cure at the expense of his Highness Prince
Adolph von Schwarzenberg, and that a similar
work of humanity has been undertaken by you in
regard to soldiers who, during the past winter,
have sought relief from their sufferings.

"The Ministry of War fully recognises your
great services and disinterested help to these

---

* This institution, called "Mecklenburgh House," because
it had originally been constructed for the Grand Duke of
Mecklenburgh, and which I saw during my visit to Graefenberg, is still carried on successfully.

soldiers, and wishes to express its gratitude to you.

"During the absence of the Minister of War,
"His representative,
"DEGENFELDT."

For the establishment of an Imperial Court of Justice at Freiwaldau, Priessnitz gave a considerable sum of money. This patriotic act was acknowledged by an autograph letter of thanks from the Minister of Justice, Von Schmerling, which reads as follows:

"VIENNA,
"*June* 12, 1850.

"The Imperial Administration of Justice for Moravia and Silesia has notified to me the active part that the population of Troppau are taking in forming the new Law Courts for these districts, and their generous contributions to that effect.

"I seize with pleasure the opportunity to express my warmest thanks to you for the sacrifice you have made by helping so largely to carry out this patriotic work.

"SCHMERLING."

In July, 1850, Priessnitz was elected member of the General Committee of Commissioners of Freiwaldau. Notwithstanding his incessant occupation, he never missed a sitting. He had the well - being of his native town at heart, and endeavoured as much as lay in his power, as a member of the committee, to reduce the costs of the administration of the commons to a minimum. He disliked useless expense, and on every occasion advocated thrift.

"Without thrift there is no getting on," he used to say, and he felt satisfied when, by his energetic and thoughtful opposition, he succeeded in influencing his colleagues in the administration to withhold their votes in the matter of unnecessary expenditure. Even during the last months of his life he prevented the erection of some buildings which were to be made at the expense of the Commune fund. He declared that he was suffering from a serious and incurable disease, and that possibly his death might make a difference in the existing favourable circumstances of Graefenberg and Freiwaldau.* During these discussions, he always remained calm and collected, never losing his temper, however much vexed and agitated he might have felt at certain moments.

Priessnitz practised courtesy from habit and · conviction. Nobody could ever accuse him of having said anything harsh or unpleasant to anyone, and his manners were unaffected and full of calm dignity. He never interrupted when

* He referred, no doubt, to the consequences of the injuries received in his youth, already mentioned.

conversing with anybody, and his answers were always clear and concise; when talking on any special subject, he riveted the attention, and kept up the interest of his listeners. He understood better than anyone how to get on with almost every class of people. He never hesitated when answering professional questions. Like most men of genius, the response seemed to come without effort, generally, as the saying is, hitting the nail on the head.

Although he was wont to clothe his thoughts in a simple and homely garb, he often gave utterance to profound truths, which, scientifically expressed, would have sounded grandiloquent. One of his favourite axioms, which he was fond of repeating, was: "A bad tool cannot do good work," which, translated into medical language, would be: "An unsound organ cannot act properly."

Priessnitz possessed a keen sense of humour. In fact, his wit had occasionally a sharp edge, although his kindness of heart prevented his saying anything harshly, or wounding people's feelings. The following anecdotes may serve as examples:

Count F., who was no stranger to the many vagaries of hypochondria, remarked one day to Priessnitz: "My dear sir, in your place, I would make short work of all hypochondriacs." Smilingly

55

Priessnitz answered: "In that case, I should be obliged to begin with your Excellency."

The year 1848 had thrown its dark shadow on the colony of Graefenberg. Many disquieting rumours came from all sides. One night after twelve o'clock the alarm bell of Freiwaldau resounded loudly over the sleeping neighbourhood. Patients, armed and unarmed, rushed out of their houses, everybody was in a state of excitement. People had been fearing for some days an assault on the spinnery of Schoenberg by some revolutionary rabble of the neighbouring districts. In the midst of the general confusion Priessnitz remained calm, and after having restored some order, he organized a patrol, at the head of which, armed only with a stout stick, he sallied forth to encounter the rioters.

After several hours' vain search in every direction, Priessnitz came to the conclusion that they had all been made victims of a hoax, and with a sarcastic smile on his lips he led his patients back to Graefenberg.

In January, 1850, a Baroness von —— was attacked with small-pox. Quite covered with the rash, and greatly suffering, Priessnitz found her in bed. Without asking many questions, he ordered compresses and packs to be administered in a certain order, besides plenty of fresh air. Some compresses he ordered to be made with special care, and on leaving called out to the maids: " Be sure not to forget the compresses, otherwise your mistress will get ill."

In 1851 a youth had been lying ill at a hospital in Bohemia for more than six weeks. As he did not get any better he expressed the wish to be treated by Priessnitz, and was conveyed with much trouble and great care to Freiwaldau. Priessnitz, who had seen the young man some months previously full of life and vigour, could not refrain from showing his surprise in beholding him almost worn to a skeleton. He calmly prescribed for him, only remarking cursorily : " The Bohemians are clever fellows : they keep the flesh and send me the bones."

A young man of careless habits left behind him debts of a compromising character. After his departure from Graefenberg, the father of the young man wrote to Priessnitz, trying to find all kinds of empty excuses to shield his son's conduct, at the same time not meeting the obligations the latter had incurred. Priessnitz sent a reply containing the following advice:

" Order two strong men to give to yourself and to your son a thorough good whipping, and for each blow dealt to your son, have *two* given to yourself."

Two women belonging to the lower middle-class had come to Graefenberg to seek relief, not from any affection of the tongue, but from some other kind of disease. They lived, it is true, together in a cottage, but were not united by the affection which alone can make life pleasant. They never could meet without quarrelling. One day, one of them, unable to bear her friend's temper any longer, came full of excitement to Priessnitz to ask for his help. Priessnitz listened calmly to the torrent of angry words with which she gave vent to her injured feelings. Finally, perfectly seriously, and without moving a muscle of his face, he said in reply to he rquestion " What *am* I to do, Herr Priessnitz?": " In future, when a cause of disagreement arises between you and your friend, instantly take some cold water into your mouth."

To another bad-tempered lady who used to torment her husband with unkind, cutting speeches, he gave the advice frequently to take cold water into her mouth, and to keep it there as long as possible.

Priessnitz was essentially a man of action. As such he detested half measures or procrastination of any kind. If a thing was to be done, he did it at once, and without hesitation. Letters, if ever so many, had to be answered the same day.

Priessnitz did not admire abstract knowledge; in fact, he did not value it sufficiently. He only respected men who combined thorough knowledge with practical worth, and his most sincere veneration was given to those rare natures who, in addition, show greatness of soul and a strong character. A true man himself, Priessnitz possessed manly courage. He showed this in his frequent nightly solitary journeys, and in the dangers he encountered so often while exercising the duties of his calling.

During the last ten years of his life Priessnitz was inundated with all kinds of presents by grateful patients in the shape of busts, portraits and pictures.

We will only mention one of these, a charming and highly-finished painting, the gift of a Frenchman, who valued it especially as being the work of his own much-loved sister. In the letter which accompanied the present, this man of delicate tact and feeling said: "This small picture is the most precious thing I possess; take it, dear and honoured Mr. Priessnitz, as the expression of my undying gratitude to you, who restored me to health. I wish it were in my power to endow you with immortality, so as to ensure your constant services to the human race, whose good genius you are."

In the year 1838 the entire district of Freiwaldau had only one single letter-carrier to do the whole of the service. He went twice a week from Freiwaldau to Johannesburg, and took the letters from those two towns to Zuckmantel, which boasted of the only Imperial Post Office for the Austrian part of the principality of Neisse.

Through Priessnitz a considerable change was brought about in these arrangements. The celebrated physician was sought by a number of people, who wanted either to be treated by him or to simply make his acquaintance. Soon the letter-carrier gave place to an Imperial letter collection. This also proved insufficient after a short time, and the necessity for a special post-office at Freiwaldau became apparent. The Imperial postmaster employed six horses in the beginning, but after a few years was obliged to keep at least twenty horses to carry on the daily service with Hahnstadt and Neisse.

Freiwaldau, which had not paid anything hitherto to the Imperial Austrian Post, now added considerably to its revenue.

During the six months from June 1 till November 30 of the year 1851, a net profit of 5,673 florins was handed over to the Imperial Government by the Freiwaldau postmaster.

The poor relief fund of Freiwaldau, at the time of Priessnitz's death, possessed a capital of more than 14,000 florins, and this considerable sum of money for so small a town was owing to Priessnitz's personal charity and beneficent influence in general. The poor in Boehmischdorf, his wife's native town, owed a great deal to him, and when the good monks of Teschen told, with tears of gratitude in their eyes, of those kind people who had helped them to collect large sums of money with which they brought relief to many hundreds of sufferers, they remembered as foremost amongst them the noble master of Graefenberg.

The concentration in a small village of persons of all nationalities,* of all ranks of society, from the cultured to the simple, with the peculiar mode of living, made Graefenberg during the space of twenty years one of the most extra-ordinary spots in the civilized world. It opened a large field of observation and varied experience of high interest to the philosopher, as well as to the man of the world and the philanthropist.

The visitors' list of the year 1846 contains the following :

From Lower Austria, 90 ; from Hungary, 73 ;

* A medical man staying at Graefenberg says : " In the year 1842 the number of patients amounted to about twelve hundred. This group was composed of Austrians, Prussians, Russians, Poles, etc., and among them forty-six English, which latter comprised Sir Augustus d'Este, General Sir John Wilson, Colonel Bowen, four English physicians, etc."

R. T. Claridge, Esq. (" Hydropathy ; or, the Water-Cure as practised by V. Priessnitz," 1842), in his preface says :

" That the aid of this *second Hippocrates* has been sought from 1829 to the present time (1842) by upwards of seven thousand invalids, the greater part of whom were of the better orders of society.

" We constantly wished that certain noble characters in our own country whom we knew to be suffering from chronic complaints were acquainted with this mode of treatment, being fully persuaded that they would be radically cured if they adopted it."

from Bohemia, 50 ; from Styria, 16 ; from Croatia, 3 ; from Transylvania, 2 ; from Tyrol, 1 ; from Prussia, 225 ; from Hamburg, 72 ; from Bavaria, 9 ; from Saxony, 6 ; from Wurtemberg, 1 ; from the rest of Germany, 21 ; from England, 107 ; from Scotland, 8 ; from Ireland, 4 ; from Russian Poland, 141 ; from Russia, 42 ; from Denmark, 28 ; from Italy, 26 ; from Turkey, 19 ; from France, 11 ; from Belgium, 4 ; from Switzerland, 4 ; from Sweden, 3 ; from Portugal, 3 ; from Wallachia, 2 ; from Greece, 1 ; from Norway, 1 ; from Australia, 1 ; from America, 18 visitors.

In the year 1847 the Graefenberg list was as follows :

From Moravia, 33 ; Bohemia, 78 ; Poland, 156 ; Silesia, 30 ; Austria, 133 ; Prussia, 187 ; Hamburg, 52 ; Styria, 13 ; Saxony, 7 ; Mecklenburg, 4 ; Bavaria, 3 ; rest of Germany, 28 ; Hungary, 112 ; Croatia, 4 ; Transylvania, 3 ; Wallachia, 4 ; Russia, 37 ; Slavonia, 5 ; Italy, 40 ; England, 94 ; Scotland, 7 ; Ireland, 2 ; France, 13 ; Switzerland, 2 ; Denmark, 22 ; Sweden, 3 ; Norway, 1 ; Belgium, 3 ; Holland, 1 ; Finland, 1 ; Lapland, 3 ; Spain, 3 ; Turkey, 4 ; North America, 29 ; Brazil, 1 ; Peru, 2 ; Egypt, 4 ; Arabia, 1 visitor. During the years 1849, 1850, and 1851, the number of yearly visitors varied from 1,100 to 1,400.

CHAPTER V

Closing Years: 1848—1851

A S we have remarked already, Priessnitz's
business began early in the day and ended
late. In the evening he liked to gather round
him some of the older patients, and to listen to
their reading aloud if the articles were not long-
winded and high-flown. The conversation on
these evenings was often interesting and attractive.
If Priessnitz made any remarks, they were generally short and to the point, and showed an original
and powerful mind, as well as a profound knowledge of human nature and keen observation.

Priessnitz was a conscientious Roman Catholic,
and was without prejudice against those belonging
to other denominations. He considered religion
indispensable to every right - thinking human
being.

He was an excellent husband and father. To
appreciate the full extent of his considerate and
winning disposition, one had to see him at home

in the midst of his family. How happy he was when surrounded by the faithful companion of his life, his six daughters, and his only son! How he valued every hour he could spend in their society! These happy hours were but too few. His professional duties deprived him of the enjoyment of those hours which are generally sacred to family intercourse.

Priessnitz was not able to attend to the education of his children, neither could his wife take charge of them, her whole time being devoted to the management of the extensive establishments. He was much concerned at his inability in this grave matter, and tried long and in vain to find a lady to whose care he could conscientiously entrust the education of his daughters. At last he was fortunate enough, through his profession, to meet with the very person for whom he had sought so long.

Miss Rosalie Kaltfeld, who had been governess in a nobleman's family, came to Graefenberg in the year 1841 for the water-cure. There she made the acquaintance of the family, and became a great favourite with every member of the Priessnitz household.

Priessnitz decided to engage her as governess to his children, and he never had cause to repent of this step, for she more than fulfilled all his expectations. With the exception of the two elder daughters, Sophie and Theresa, the other children were all educated at Johannesburg, and came only on high festivals to Graefenberg with their governess.

Priessnitz's only son, Vincent Paul Priessnitz, when quite a boy, showed a special predilection for cold water. Whenever he felt unwell, he was quite ready to become his own physician, prescribing either a cold compress, a dripping-sheet, or some other application. He was able to distinguish the effect of each of these with accuracy, and to say to his nurse when the occasion occurred: "I want a dripping-sheet. I must have another compress. That does me good."

In the summer of 1851 little Vincent had the small-pox, and the father, sure of succeeding, treated the child with cold water, having saved a great number of patients from that malignant disease. Vincent got well, and was stronger and better than before.

During the cure, the little boy, only four years old, showed more courage, and was more reasonable, than many a grown-up person.

Vincent Paul Priessnitz died in early manhood, leaving two children—one son, the present owner of the Priessnitz property at Graefenberg, and a daughter.

The only other grandchild is the daughter of

Colonel Ripper, mentioned in this biography, and of Marie (*née* Priessnitz), his wife.

Accompanying this chapter are the portraits of all Priessnitz's children and children by marriage, as well as of the grandchildren, of whom only one (Colonel Ripper's daughter) is married at the present time.

Priessnitz's last days were a fit ending to such a nobly-spent life. Since his illness in the year 1847 Priessnitz had failed to recover his usual health. The exigencies of his arduous calling never left him sufficient time for thorough rest. He was affected by the baneful influences of the terrible years of 1848-49. The wickedness, the hypocrisy, the evidences of every kind of immorality—of which the history of those years gives so many instances—had a crushing effect on his whole being, and he lost his equanimity of mind and even of temper.

He became depressed, and looked on affairs in general from the dark side. The welfare of the middle classes seemed to him seriously imperilled, and the future full of danger for all ranks of society.

" Truth and confidence are no more." " People are no longer taught to obey." " Those in authority have forgotten how to deal out punishment with justice, or to reward merit where it is due."

These sentiments he expressed frequently to

(7) Vincenz Paul Priessnitz.   (8) Wilhelmina Priessnitz.

(9) Hans Ripper.

(10) Marie Ripper

(11) Paul von Dessewffy.

(12) Bertha von Dessewffy.

(13) Sofie von Ujhazy.

(14) Josi von Ujhazy.

(1) Otto, Baron von Uslar-Gleichen.

(2) Anna, Baroness von Uslar-Gleichen.

(3) Victor Skunowitsch.

(4) Antonia Skunowitsch.

(5) Albert von Ujhazy.

(6) Therese von Ujhazy.

V. PRIESSNITZ' DAUGHTERS AND SON AND SONS- AND DAUGHTER-IN-LAW.

To face p. 66.

those about him. In vain some of his friends tried to draw his attention to signs of improvement which occasionally made themselves felt amidst the general darkness and confusion. He persisted in saying: "If God does not help, everything must go to ruin."

Under such injurious influences Priessnitz passed the year from the winter of 1850 to the following winter of 1851, the former being an unusually mild one. Notwithstanding the favourable weather, he said to one of his patients : " Never has a winter been so trying to me."

Priessnitz soon realized that his life was seriously threatened. He remarked to one of his oldest friends, Landrath Spinner, who out of respectful gratitude often came to stay with him : " I believe that the end is approaching; I do not think that my complaint can be cured."

A bad cough, which seized him each time he took his bath early in the morning, caused anxiety to his friends. Notwithstanding the weak state of his health, Priessnitz was as assiduous in the discharge of his professional duties as during his best days. At last, at the instance of his family, he subjected himself to special treatment, which benefited him, but did not restore to him the looks of a healthy man.

In July, 1851, Priessnitz declared that from the following November he should be obliged to give

up attending patients at Freiwaldau. "I can do
no more," he told one of his patients who lived
in the town, "otherwise I shall ruin myself completely, and then shall be unable to help anybody." After repeated remarks on his part of a
similar nature, a feeling of concern spread through
the neighbourhood of Graefenberg. The inhabitants of Freiwaldau still hoped that the misfortune
might be averted by united entreaties on their
part. In October, 1851, Dr. Selinger came by
special invitation to see his friend. He found
Priessnitz much altered, pale, emaciated, and
considerably aged. During his guest's stay he
rallied somewhat, and was cheerful and talkative.

Those last days at Graefenberg remained a
treasured memory to Dr. Selinger, who had the
privilege of spending them with his never-to-be-
forgotten friend.

The news of Miss Kaltfeld's serious illness at
Budamir, whither she had gone with all the
Priessnitz children, except little Vincent, on a
visit to his eldest daughter, Sophie, upset the
anxious father, who exclaimed: "My God, what
will become of my children if she dies!" The
suspense, however, did not last long, for after
three days a reassuring letter came to inform him
that his daughter had undertaken the treatment
of the case, and saved the patient's life. The

(1) Wilma Priessnitz.   (2) Vincenz Priessnitz.
(3) Captain Hans Friedrich.   (4) Zdenka Friedrich.

To face p. 68

letter contained besides all the details of the cure, and Priessnitz, full of just pride, exclaimed joyfully: "Sophie has presence of mind. She has done well !"

On October 7, the day of farewell to his friend, Dr. Selinger felt deeply and strangely moved. He repeatedly pressed Priessnitz to his heart with these words: "May God keep and bless you, dear Priessnitz !" "If I get through the winter," he replied, "I shall last a long while yet. Goodbye, and God bless you !"

He did not get through the winter: the end was not far off then. They never saw each other again alive.

On October 8 Priessnitz felt so ill that he went to bed. After several days, during which he prescribed for himself, he became better and got up, but a relapse soon followed. The patients' constant demand upon his strength did not leave him sufficient rest and quiet. His wife's anxiety having now become so great, she wrote for her children to return home at once, and on October 23 they all came, including the eldest daughter, Frau von Ujhazy.

It is impossible to paint the feelings of joy and of sadness as one child after another was folded in the loving father's embrace, and for the moment the latter seemed to forget his sufferings in the happiness of reunion with his dear ones. This happy change lasted for some days; the patient seemed to improve hourly, and was able, after a few days, to appear in the large hall, where his presence was greeted with joy. He came on three consecutive evenings. On the third evening he looked wonderfully well, and was unusually cheerful and talkative. He spoke a great deal about the new building which he was going to undertake in 1852, and of which the plans had already been prepared. After some remarks on the building he said: "I am going to treat myself thoroughly; if eruptions on the skin show themselves (crisis), I can yet get well; if not, there will be no building."

On the next day he went early in the morning to Johannesburg to transact some business. The day was damp and foggy. He returned late at night, having caught a chill, and went to bed, feeling unwell. Soon after a swelling showed itself on the feet, which made him anxious. He again took to his bed. He got up several times during the day, and in order to get warm after a cold bath, went from his room on the first-floor to one on the ground-floor to saw some wood.

His wife and two elder daughters, who principally took care of their dear invalid, could not always hide their anxiety when in his presence. It made him unhappy to witness their sadness and their tear-stained faces, and he repeatedly said: " Do not fret, my beloved ones, I shall get well again. Is there not a God in heaven, and cold water to help me ?"

Nevertheless, he grew weaker and weaker, while his eyes shone with an almost supernatural gleam. One day, his wife, fearing the worst, asked him whether he would like to see a doctor. " No," Priessnitz answered, with a clear and determined voice.

These last days showed how devoted he was to his principles. Notwithstanding rapidly-increasing exhaustion, he cheerfully prescribed for every patient who came to consult him. On the eve of his death his wife again asked him: "Dear husband, shall I send for a doctor?" "No, dear child," he again said, with the utmost calm, but without hesitation.

On November 28, 1851, he wanted to go downstairs at five o'clock in the morning to saw wood after his cold bath, but yielding to his wife's entreaties not to go down, she had the wood and appliances for sawing brought into his sitting-room, and about nine o'clock he went once more to the sawing-machine to warm himself, but soon pushed it aside, saying: "Take that away; I shall not require it any more." These pathetic words made the most painful impression on the assembled family. About two o'clock in the afternoon the poor wife stood near the bed where her fast-sinking husband lay, asking in a voice full of

repressed despair: "Will you not see a doctor ?"
A scarcely audible "No" came from the lips of
the dying man.

A few minutes after four o'clock he suddenly
got up from his couch, dressed himself in a long,
warm gown, and seated himself perfectly upright
upon a chair near the window. There once
more he looked out upon the beautiful hillside
woods, which during his whole life he had
deeply loved, and his spirit seemed entirely lost
in thought. A little later he shivered, and asked
to be rubbed with a wet sheet, and then with very
little assistance went back to his bed. Scarcely
had he been placed in a horizontal position when
the muscles of the left side of the face and his
hands became convulsed — a last breath — and
Priessnitz was dead. The soul of one of the
noblest of men had returned to its Creator.

Priessnitz left a clause in his will desiring a
post-mortem examination of his body. Several
doctors and many of the patients were present at
this ceremony.

The left lung was found to be affected, the liver
abnormal, the kidneys also diseased. The brain
was found to be of considerable weight, and beautifully shaped. The cause of the internal havoc
was probably the accident which he had in his
youth, when the heavy van passed over his body

and broke his ribs. Until then he had been, according to his sister's declaration, a perfectly sound and healthy boy.

The day of the funeral was retarded, owing to circumstances which necessitated rather complicated arrangements.

The patients decided to send a deputation, chosen from amongst their own number, to the Prince-Bishop of Breslau, to invite him to officiate at the funeral, which they wished to be as impressive as possible, so as to testify to their love and veneration for their deeply-regretted physician.

His Eminence, who had been cured of terrible sufferings himself by Priessnitz's care and devotion, received the deputation, deeply moved, and regretted being unable just then to come to Freiwaldau, nor could he send his suffragan, who was lying dangerously ill himself.

The deputation returned the following day, bearing an autograph letter from his Eminence, addressed to the widow, as follows :

"*To the Afflicted Widow of Vincent Priessnitz :*

" DEAR MRS. PRIESSNITZ,

" To my great sorrow I have heard of the sudden death of our dear and honoured Priessnitz, and I cannot refrain from expressing to you my deep and heartfelt sympathy. It is, alas ! no consolation to you to know, what has certainly

73

never been said before of any man in private life, nay, scarcely of any reigning prince, that his name has gone forth to the most distant parts of the world as benefactor of the human race, and that therefore he will be mourned by thousands and hundreds of thousands. Your loss being shared by so many only testifies to the magnitude of your misfortune. As a true Christian woman, however, you know from whom to seek help and comfort, and I pray that God may give you and your family strength and courage to submit to His will without murmur, and that He may reward the great and good man, now taken from us, for all he has done to alleviate the sufferings of his fellow-creatures, and for the help he has given to the poor and unfortunate ones of his native country."

On the morning of the fourth of December a large crowd of people filled the wide space in front of Priessnitz's house. From all parts of the neighbouring districts men, women and children of all classes had come to assist at the mournful ceremony, to pay the last honour to him who had at one time or another been their benefactor.

Soon after nine o'clock began the ceremony of the consecration of the body, which lasted about an hour. The coffin, covered with a velvet pall, was then carried from the house, and placed on a sledge arranged for that purpose. The family and relations of the deceased, full of grief, followed. A procession was formed. It slowly and solemnly wended its way towards Freiwaldau.

All was silence. No sound was audible save the rushing of water from the springs, which seemed to send their last farewell to him who had drawn them forth from their quiet to minister to the health of Europe. The sun, which had been hidden behind heavy clouds, now for a few moments shone radiantly on the misty landscape, soon, however, to disappear, and a heavy snowfall added to the deeply melancholy scene.

The road from Graefenberg to Freiwaldau, about three miles long, was thronged with people. The first had reached Freiwaldau before the last had left Graefenberg. The procession was formed at the entrance of the town, headed by thirty priests, and amidst the tolling of bells went to the large square in front of the parish church.

A number of inhabitants of Freiwaldau lifted the coffin from the sledge, carried it into the church, and placed it in front of the high altar. A mass for the dead was now celebrated by several priests, accompanied by beautiful music. Towards noon the mass was concluded, and the procession formed again. Twelve patients now carried the coffin into the centre of the large square, where it was taken up by twelve inhabitants of Freiwaldau, who carried it, followed by the procession, and

75

amidst the solemn sounds of appropriate music, to the cemetery.   The family and nearest relations formed a group round the grave, and behind them stood the representatives of every nation of Europe and North and South America, as well as mourners from Graefenberg, Freiwaldau, and many other towns and districts.

The priest who had conducted the procession now pronounced the benediction, and at the last words, " Requiescat in pace," patients and citizens lowered the coffin with the remains of one of the noblest of men to its resting-place.

There was no long speech to praise and exalt the merits of the deceased.   Nothing but the few words full of meaning, " Requiescat in pace," were pronounced over the remains of a man whose life had been one long act of goodness and of blessing to others, of duty and charity and love of God, which will bear fruit for all coming generations, who will each in turn from grateful hearts join in a never ending,

" REQUIESCAT IN PACE."*

* In the year 1853 Priessnitz's body was removed to the Mausoleum mentioned in one of the following chapters, where he lies beside his wife.

Mrs. Priessnitz survived her husband barely three years. Grief at her great loss had enfeebled her health, and she died of dysentery while staying in Hungary with her eldest daughter, Frau von Ujhazy.   Mrs. Priessnitz was born on September 17, 1805, and died on August 31, 1854.

MAUSOLEUM.

HOUSE WHERE PRIESSNITZ WAS BORN.

To face p. 76.

CHAPTER VI

MEDICAL VIEWS AND PROCEDURE

IT is not often that one man makes such a change in the world as Priessnitz did. We find many men who have an influence while they live, but they no sooner pass away than their influence vanishes too. In short, their influence was personal, not vital. It touched actions only, not principles. Therein we see the difference between Priessnitz and others.

What were the means which raised Priessnitz to such eminence? One is astonished at their simplicity. He did not attain this eminence by painful and unceasing plodding only, but rather by the intelligent development of all his powers, by the careful training of his heart and affections, and finally by the exercise of judgment in making use of all these gifts and acquirements.

Priessnitz took up the water-cure where the two Hahns and Oertel had left it, and thereon built up his system. The two elder doctors feared

77

that the prolonged use of cold water might cause eruptions and skin sores. Priessnitz, on the contrary, tried in many cases to cause them to appear, and after their appearance continued his treatment with perseverance until the patient showed no longer any signs of throwing out these eruptions.*

The precision with which Priessnitz diagnosed surprised many patients. They looked upon him almost as one endowed with supernatural power.

Let me give here a few instances of his judgment:

A gentleman from Vienna had called together a number of eminent physicians to have a consultation on the state of his health. The doctors were unanimous in advising him to try the water-cure, and wrote down an opinion of his case. With this document in his pocket the patient arrived at Graefenberg. He gave a short account of his illness without mentioning the medical opinion. Priessnitz, without replying, looked steadily at him for several minutes, and then gave utterance to exactly the same opinion at which the doctors had arrived after four hours of earnest deliberation. Full of admiration, the sufferer exclaimed: " How is it possible ?"

* Sir Charles Scudamore on " The ' Crisis' in the Water-Cure " (" Water-Cure Journal," Malvern, vol. i., 1847-48) : " The very important matter of 'crisis' is always sought for with much solicitude by Priessnitz and patients."

Another gentleman arrived from Vienna after having been brought very low by the ordinary medical treatment he had undergone. Priessnitz listened patiently to his complaints, and said quietly: " You suffer from relaxation of the intestines. You will get well, but you must submit to all you are told, and do it." The patient did so, and soon left in perfect health.

The Chaplain of the Prussian Embassy in Rome, Von Pabst, went, according to the advice of five doctors, to Graefenberg, having been treated for affection of the liver. He arrived late one evening at Graefenberg, introduced himself in a dimly-lighted room to Priessnitz, told the history of his sufferings, and confessed that he had come under protest, and only on the doctors' advice, to try the water-cure, but that he had made up his mind to go in for it seriously. Priessnitz looked at him for awhile, and at last said: " You do not suffer from the liver only: your complaint is piles. You will see it yourself in a few weeks." The result of the treatment was as Priessnitz had predicted.

Priessnitz was never deceived by a blooming appearance as to the state of a person's health, and he gave proof of this in many instances.

One day some gentlemen were praising and admiring the great beauty and healthy appearance of a young girl who had come to stay with a suffering relative, who was undergoing the water-treatment. "Only appearance," said Priessnitz; "in a week's time that young lady will be seriously ill." He had predicted exactly what happened, and it was many months before the young girl was well again.

The following cases have been furnished by the kindness of Mr. M. B. Tristram, who was under Priessnitz in the year 1849, only two years before the founder of hydropathy died :*

A captain of artillery in the Austrian army consulted Priessnitz on some constant and severe pains in the head from which he was suffering. They were the effects of a cannon-ball passing in close proximity to that part of his body. Priessnitz informed the young officer's relations that the brain was irreparably injured, and that although the patient was able to work out abstruse mathematical problems, as before his accident, he would die suddenly before long, which he did.

An English lady, married to an Italian nobleman, came to Graefenberg to consult Priessnitz about the health of one of her daughters, supposed

* " During my forty years' practice in London, I have come in contact with a number of people who were under Priessnitz's treatment at Graefenberg, and could give endless cases did space permit. However, I give the above in preference, as Mr. Tristram, with his son and daughter, are now undergoing treatment in my establishment."—R. M., December, 1896.

to be suffering from spinal disease. On entering the room, Priessnitz at once said: "Yes, your daughter is very ill; in fact, she is so bad that I am not certain to be able to cure her." The mother interrupted him, saying: "You are mistaken: the one you are looking at is in perfect health, very strong, a good walker and rider, and has never had a day's illness in her life." "I repeat," said Priessnitz, "that this young lady is very seriously affected, and it will be advisable to let her begin the cure at once. In a fortnight's time the disease, which exists now in a latent form, will then declare itself, and she will lose the use of her limbs. As to her sister, I can promise to set her right in a very short time."

Priessnitz's prognostication was fulfilled. Fortunately, however, for the young lady, the treatment proved so successful that after a few months she was radically cured, and is living at the present time and enjoying good health.

As regards his own case, Mr. Tristram says:

"After a stay of about a year in Ceylon, I was ordered home by my doctor, being in a very bad state of health, owing to repeated attacks of malarial fever, followed by a bad attack of cholera. I joined my parents, then residing at Florence, and after a year and a half spent in that city and at the baths of Lucca, my doctor gave me up in despair, saying that he could do nothing more for me, and, in fact, I was worse than when I first went to him. He then recommended me to try the water-cure, as being the only treatment likely to benefit me.

" I was suffering from constant attacks of fever; my right arm had become almost powerless; I had an ulcerated throat, to which caustic was applied twice a week, and I was altogether broken down in health at the age of twenty-three. I started for Graefenberg in 1848. On addressing Priessnitz, he said that he did not require any description of my symptoms, but that he would see me in my bath the next morning. Accordingly, I found him in the bath-room next morning. I had to plunge into a tub of cold water for a few seconds, then dry myself by flapping my sheet with the help of the bathman.

" Then Priessnitz examined me carefully, not allowing me to say a word. He then told me the various ills I was suffering from, without missing a single one. I was ordered a wet-sheet pack, followed by a plunge into the big tub. That was early in the morning. At 11 a.m. I had to take a cold hip-bath for twenty minutes. In the afternoon I had a rubbing with a dripping-sheet for several minutes. I was ordered to go bare-necked and very slightly clad, and after my treatment had to walk briskly out of doors to obtain a good reaction. Towards the latter end of my cure I took a douche of icy-cold water, falling in a stream from a height of twelve feet. I was completely cured at the end of a little over two months. I remained, however, a whole year at Graefenberg, finding the life and society so pleasant, and the place suiting me so well. I found there people from all countries, and amongst them many of my own countrymen. I had, therefore, many opportunities of judging hydropathic treatment, which left no doubt in my mind as to its great value.

" I was amazed at Priessnitz's extraordinary ability in diagnosing human ailments, and at his power of adapting the treatment to suit each chronic case that came to him."

Priessnitz's mode of diagnosing his cases was unique. He always superintended the administration of the first treatment given to a patient of either sex, and in the majority of cases he prescribed the treatment there and then, without again attending personally to the treatment. In difficult cases, however, he frequently saw the treatment given, in order to observe the reactionary powers of the skin.

I must say, judging from my own experience, that nothing will afford a hydropathic practitioner so much evidence of how the patient is progressing as observing the skin while undergoing treatment, and I am convinced that the success of Priessnitz was due to his keen and penetrating power of observation, coupled with his individual attention to patients.

The observations which Priessnitz made at the first bath enabled him to decide whether the patient was fit or unfit for the water-cure. If the skin, after the bath, was warm and supple, and if the patient felt comfortable and refreshed, he was a good subject for the cure. If, on the contrary, the patient's skin remained dry and cold after the first bath, and failed to show any heightened activity, or if the patient felt weak and exhausted, or his suffering limbs remained insensible to the touch, then these symptoms were deemed of bad augury for his progress towards health.*

Simultaneously with the recognition of a disease, there arose in Priessnitz's mind a distinct idea of the mode of treatment in each case.

Priessnitz says : " When I examine a patient's appearance, especially his eyes and his skin, I see before me a picture, so to say, of his diseased state ; I *see* what is the matter with him, and at the same time the exact means to overcome the disease which causes his sufferings. I then prescribe accordingly."

His prescriptions were given verbally in presence of the attendants. Both patient and attendant

---

* These cases, which were a difficulty with Priessnitz, are now easily and successfully dealt with by the use of hot-air baths as a preliminary to general cold treatment.

(1) Attendant Habicht.   (2) Anna Stiller.   (3) Matern Priessnitz.
(4) Josef Hackenberg.   (5) Pauline Koenig.

To face p. 84.

were under obligation faithfully to carry out these orders. The attendant was forbidden to listen to any objections or remonstrances from the patient, who was only allowed any change in the treatment by the express orders of Priessnitz himself. It was the attendant's duty also to report any deviation or non-observance on the patient's part. If anybody showed signs of insubordination to these rules, or did he return to his old and prejudicial ways of living, or, worse still, tried some new method of his own, Priessnitz told him kindly of the danger of doing so. When, however, these remonstrances were ignored, the unruly visitor was requested to leave the establishment.

The number of visits which Priessnitz paid to his patients was determined by the nature and gravity of their disease. If the malady was not very serious or deep-seated, their doctor's first visit was often his last.

In serious cases his patients could always count on Priessnitz's careful and devoted attention. He then came often, and it was deeply interesting to watch the gifted man's behaviour on those occasions. Silently he listened to the loudest complaints, and if they were the result of imaginary evils or self-indulgent habits, he prescribed calmly and firmly the necessary treatment.

Patients who showed no energy to overcome

difficulties, persons of cowardly disposition, with no strength of will or self-control, were not his favourites, and he respected them but little. "To use the water-cure, a person must have force of will," he was wont to say. "Those who have a weak character, or show no inclination to strengthen it, had better remain away from the water-cure." Of a lady who was not disposed to submit to certain necessary hardships, and thought the fare much too simple, he said : "She would like me to offer her the whole water-cure in a coffee-cup !"

True suffering met with sincere and warm sympathy from Priessnitz. He tried by kind and encouraging words to reconcile the sufferer to the discomforts and hardships of the treatment. "It is true," he often said, "my patients have a hard time of it, but one cannot do too much for one's health."

Priessnitz was admirable in moments of danger ; he then displayed an unfailing energy, nursing the sufferer himself if necessary, and preserving an unalterable calm and confidence, which had the happiest effect on the patient's mind, giving him courage and confidence in his physician's ability.

In some cases he was like one inspired. Let me give a few instances :

Mrs. E., who visited Graefenberg in the year 1839, suffered from chronic vertigo. One day the cry was heard: "Mrs. E. is dead; she has had an epileptic attack!" The lady had fallen unconscious to the ground on the way to her apartment and was cold and rigid. Priessnitz, who had hastened to the spot, had her carried to her room, put in a bath, and rubbed with wetted hands uninterruptedly by four persons, adding his own personal help. After five hours' unceasing rubbing the tired-out attendants exclaimed: "It is useless: she is dead!" "No," replied Priessnitz calmly, "she is *not* dead, but life is ebbing away. Continue your work!" And until long after midnight the rubbing was continued, when Priessnitz, feeling the pulse, joyfully exclaimed: "The victory is ours! Only go on rubbing; at about three o'clock she will become conscious."

About that hour Mrs. E. awoke. Soon after she took some exercise in the fresh morning air, dined in the large hall, and enjoyed good health for many years after.

In one of the most distant houses of the colony one of Priessnitz's special friends lay dangerously ill with typhus fever. One evening, notwithstanding every effort, he became worse and worse. Priessnitz began to despair of his recovery, and expressed the opinion to those present that death would most likely ensue the same night. At eleven o'clock, on Priessnitz's return home, he paced restlessly up and down his room, and at last went to bed. After a few moments' sleep he jumped out of bed, called for his horse, and hastened to the dying man's house.

Arrived there, he proceeded to give different directions, and after two hours' unceasing labour, in which he took an active part, the patient began to show some signs of mending. As soon as Priessnitz perceived this, he exclaimed: " Thank God, he is saved !"

In some critical cases Priessnitz, with full confidence in his principal remedy, did not hesitate to have recourse to heroic treatment. Amongst many others, his own child—his eldest daughter Sophie herself—was treated in this way.

She had not quite recovered from an attack of ague, when one cold night in autumn she was awakened by cries of " Fire !" The sudden shock caused her acute pains in the region of the chest. Priessnitz, who had been employed during the whole night in helping to extinguish the fire, could only after all danger was over turn his attention to his daughter. He prescribed wet packs, followed by a tepid bath, and finally a full bath of cold water. As the sufferer did not get any better, he ordered dripping-sheets and sitz-baths. But Sophie complained of increased pains and difficulty in breathing. Priessnitz now made her remain from three to four minutes in a cold bath, followed by a bath of tepid water.

This treatment was repeated very many times after each attack that day, whereupon the pains and difficulty of breathing disappeared, and the feeling of complete recovery began.

Most of the different maladies to which men are subject, and often in their most repulsive forms, had come under Priessnitz's experience. He tried to trace innumerable diseases and infirmities to their source, and to gain distinct fundamental ideas as to the mode of treatment which ought to guide a physician. He arrived on both points at very original conclusions.*

The principal causes of disease and degeneration in Europe were, in Priessnitz's opinion, immorality and the poisoning of the system through the introduction into the stomach of mineral medicines.

Medicines administered to alleviate disease have the effect of augmenting existing trouble, because the body cannot assimilate them, and they are partially absorbed to the injury of the tissues of the body.

The physician's duty is to try to get rid of foreign matters from the body, and to substitute

---

* A distinguished medical man, while visiting Graefenberg, makes the following observations: "I hope my medical and other readers will not run away with the idea that there is no theory in Priessnitz's doings, and that it is all chance work. They could not be more mistaken. I have convinced myself at Graefenberg that Priessnitz has a reason for all he does."

89

sound and healthy matter, and thus to enable the human body to perform its functions regularly and without hindrance. This can best be done by suitable food, air, exercise, rest and water, which are the natural requirements of man.

" The human body must be strengthened and not weakened," said Priessnitz. " When the body is sufficiently strong, it allows no pernicious matters to remain in the system : it throws them out."*

Priessnitz had not allowed his son to be vaccinated. He considered vaccination an encroachment on Nature's salutary ways, and therefore as a misfortune for mankind. " Small-pox," he said, " is only dangerous and disfiguring because people are wrongly treated. Vaccination seldom

* Edward Johnson, M.D., in his "Theory and Principles of Hydropathy" (1852), draws an interesting parallel between Baron Liebig and Priessnitz, showing how they both came to the same conclusion as regards some of the great general truths on the principles of hydropathy. He says : "The most elaborate experiments and a vast amount of the most scientific learning have taught Liebig ; strong powers of general reasoning. acute observation, and long experience have taught Priessnitz. The two have arrived at the same goal by different roads. Priessnitz cannot give to his knowledge a scientific expression ; but when Priessnitz declares, as he does, that the application of cold water cures diseases by strengthening general health and fortifying the system, and when Liebig declares, as he does, that the abstraction of heat cures diseases by exalting and accelerating the transformation of tissues, the two do but give expression to the same fact in different language."

eliminates from the system the noxious matter accumulated therein. This matter is the foundation of scrofula, herpetic eruptions, hip disease, and other complaints. Those who have been vaccinated easily fall victims to those diseases. To anyone who disbelieves my statement, I am ready to show thousands of letters to prove the truth of it."

"Physicians abroad," he continued, "do not believe that small-pox has ever been seen at Graefenberg; neither do they believe that this disease can be cured with cold water. There are, however, several medical men whom I have called on purpose to witness the proceedings, and they can confirm the fact of small-pox cases at Graefenberg, and also that I have cured them all; that never a small-pox patient has died here; that there has never been any disfigurement; and, further, that every symptom of the special illness for which these persons came to Graefenberg disappeared at the same time."

On being questioned how he treated these patients, he replied: "I usually had them put, three times a day, into linen sheets wrung out of cold water, and changed every thirty minutes until the fever abated; then had them bathed in tepid water (62° to 64° Fahr.). I gave the patients good nourishing diet and cold water to drink. They were, of course, at liberty to change their linen, but the windows had to remain open. With this treatment the sick ones all recovered, and scarcely ever an attendant caught the disease."

Simple as Priessnitz's fundamental ideas were, the means which he employed in his treatment, and by which he effected the marvellous cures, have since astonished the world. These means, in connection with those ideas, were : Cold water, adequate food, exercise in the open air, and rubbing with the flat hand.

Next to fresh air and light, Priessnitz found his principal healing agent in water. He saw no growth, no well-being, no life, without water. In scientific knowledge of the chemical components of this so-called element there were many far in advance of him ; but no one in the world could touch him as regards an intimate knowledge of the effects of water upon the animal organism. His vast experience had revealed to him the great healing-power of water, and his desire to serve humanity by alleviating its sufferings had shown him the varied ways in which it might be applied.

In some cases he made use of it in order to dissolve certain matters, in others to strengthen and to soothe the system, and, in others again, he used it with great success to allay inflammation. He prescribed water to be taken internally as well as applied externally.

As a beverage, cold water is refreshing to the

human body. It dilutes the blood, refreshes and purifies it, stimulates the appetite, and promotes digestion, dissolves foreign matters, and vivifies the whole organism.

Priessnitz recommended the drinking of cold water, and in some cases prescribed large quantities of it.

Externally, he brought the water in contact with the body in various ways : by means of douches, cold full-baths, tepid and sitz-baths, foot, head and eye baths, and other partial baths. Also through packing in wet-sheets, compresses, bandages, and finally through injections.

The cold-water bath in the large bath and the douche he prescribed in cases where he wanted to give a shock to the whole system, and bring about a better circulation. The douche he ordered specially in deep-seated affections, in obstinate cases of insufficient circulation, and to bring about a crisis.

When he wanted to quiet the cerebro-spinal nerves by accelerating the circulation in the abdomen, he usually ordered a tepid or cold sitz-bath. If his object was to bring the blood to the surface so as to obtain a good reaction in an anæmic or weakly body, he prescribed a rubbing with the wet-sheet, accompanied by friction. A linen sheet, dipped in cold water, was well wrung out and put round the patient, who was in an upright position, and who had wetted previously his face and chest. The attendant then rubbed, quickly and briskly, each separate part. The packing in wet-sheets generally preceded water ablutions. It served to soothe the body as well as to draw out noxious matters. It had, besides, the object of promoting the action of the skin, and thus making the after-bath more effective. The sheets the patients were packed in, after having been used, were frequently marked with different coloured spots, and had a strong and most offensive odour.

If a patient suffered from a hard and dry skin, or was inclined to be feverish, Priessnitz ordered several packs to succeed each other before the bath. For the pack a thick blanket was spread over the mattress, a well-wrung-out sheet put on the top, the patient tightly wrapped in this sheet and blanket, besides being carefully covered with more blankets, and thus left for thirty or forty minutes.

The waist bandage, which had rendered Priessnitz such good service in his youth after his serious accident, was prescribed to all who suffered from complaints in the abdominal regions. In fact, nearly all his patients had to wear this bandage to facilitate digestion, and aid the action of the bowels, and to draw to the surface rashes—in other words, a crisis.

This bandage, called " Neptune's belt " by the

patients, was a linen or cotton strip a little over a quarter of a yard wide, and long enough to go three times round the body. A third part of it is wrung tightly out of cold water. When dry, it is re-wetted, and is in many cases worn night and day. Many adherents of the water - cure continue to wear these bandages long after they have left Graefenberg. If Priessnitz discerned some local trouble which was not merely a symptom of some other disease, but independent thereof (as cystic tumours), he ordered cold compresses. The compress has the same effect on each separate part as the pack has on the whole body: it tends to draw deleterious matter to the surface.

Notwithstanding the great apparent simplicity of these various applications, it is not easy to choose in each case the appropriate one.

Priessnitz scarcely ever failed in choosing the right one.

Through Priessnitz, who tried the curative effects of cold water on himself, and on many thousands of patients, the water-cure has been, and will be, handed down to posterity.

CHAPTER VII

MEDICAL VIEWS AND PROCEDURE—*continued*.

PRIESSNITZ resorted extensively to rubbing with the flat hand. He recognised the beneficial effects of manipulative friction as a curative agent.

Personally, Priessnitz exercised a powerful influence on his patients, both by his look and by the touch of his hand.

One of his earnest looks was sufficient to make a spoiled and enervated patient do things without a murmur which under ordinary circumstances, and under another doctor, would have called forth energetic opposition, and even hysterical attacks.

There were, of course, many cases in which Priessnitz, neither with his hands nor by any other means, was able to succeed in doing good. But as long as there remained hope, this man, of essentially practical mind, tried to help the sufferer, and many owed their lives to his untiring energy. A Countess T. was amongst the number.

This lady had been given up by her doctors, and was on her way to Graefenberg as a last hope. She had arrived at Freiwaldau in such a state of collapse as to cause fears that her illness might at any moment terminate fatally. Priessnitz, with the help of attendants, tried in vain to restore vitality to her rigid body, using means which had proved successful in similar cases. Suddenly he asked the countess's maid how her mistress had felt during the journey. On hearing that the lady had been comparatively well, he at once ordered a carriage. The sufferer was carefully put into it, and driven about for several hours in the night air. Before her return consciousness was restored, and the countess was so far recovered as to allow Priessnitz to begin the actual treatment. The means he now employed proved so successful, that a few months later the lady had completely recovered, and eventually became the mother of several healthy children.

The extreme simplicity of the treatment has misled many. Such prescribe, perhaps with the help of a printed manual, for themselves and others. Bitter disappointment has often been the result of such proceedings. After very few experiments, it will become apparent to anyone that the hydropathic treatment must be regulated by the requirements of every individual case. It is not a matter of small importance how to apply water. For instance, a headache can be cured by applying cold water; but whether to use a foot-bath or a head-bath or a compress has to be determined by the origin of the headache, whether it proceeds from local anæmia, or from too plentiful feeding, from a chill, or from over-heating, whether from too much or too little sleep. Many an enthusiastic believer in the water-cure has been turned against it through his own injudicious treatment. Priessnitz often complained about this matter, and argued against books on the water-cure being used by the public.

A doctor in Breslau had treated two children suffering from scarlet fever with cold water so clumsily that both died, and the unhappy father published the whole case in a leading paper. One of his patients read this article to Priessnitz, asking him if he knew Dr. B. " Oh yes," was the reply; " he has been at Graefenberg some time, to study the water-cure."

" If all your pupils are like him, they cannot give you much satisfaction," remarked another visitor.

" It is too vexing," said Priessnitz: "it is always professors of medicine who are my worst pupils."

There is not much harm done in dabbling with water in slight matters, such as contusions or bruises, but it is very different in serious cases, where a crisis is brought about by the efforts of the internal organs to eject noxious matters from the body. The symptoms preceding a crisis are often alarming to the layman. The patient feels very uncomfortable, becomes depressed, and loses his appetite, complains of sleeplessness, of hot and cold shivers, and often is seized with violent fever. The novice in hydropathy loses presence of mind in such cases; the non-medical man becomes completely helpless; the doctor has recourse to his accustomed remedies, without much success under existing circumstances. Priessnitz, on the contrary, showed his real greatness in these moments. However alarming or unexpected the symptoms, either before or after the crisis, might be, he never lost presence of mind, nor calmness and confidence. His vast experience had taught him how to deal with them.* Frequently he was heard to say : " Anything brought forth by water, the water will cure !"

" It is terrible how I suffer," a patient belonging to the upper classes said one day. " My nerves

---

* John Gibbs, " Letters from Graefenberg ": It is principally in the treatment of these symptoms that Priessnitz should be seen ; then his tact, his penetration, his presence of mind, and his master hand, cannot but excite feelings of admiration ; then will be displayed his unparalleled calm assurance ; then he will show how successfully he can master the storm and distance the danger, and this by means of the cold water which has caused it.

are in a perpetual state of irritation. I fear a nervous fever may ensue."

Priessnitz looked a few seconds at the faint-hearted patient, who cowered under that calm gaze, and then said smilingly: " If only you could get a good regular nervous fever, that is exactly what I have been wanting for you: that would be the best kind of crisis for you, and you would then get well in a short time."

The poor nervous patient looked tremblingly at Priessnitz, and murmured scarcely audibly: " But——"

Priessnitz instantly comforted him, saying: "You imagine you would die! Don't be afraid: nobody has yet died with me of nervous fever."

During the summer of the year 1851 a young lady of unusual beauty became blind. The whole colony deplored this misfortune, for she had endeared herself to many through the charm and sweetness of her disposition. The parents were in despair. Priessnitz tried to comfort them by assuring them that in this case it was only a crisis, and that by the autumn she would be well, and have regained her sight.

Their confidence thus restored, they waited patiently for the fulfilment of the great doctor's words. But week after week passed, and no improvement took place. The month of August had come; the hope of recovery had in the meanwhile grown fainter and fainter. On the other hand, the necessity for leaving Graefenberg became urgent. Finally, the departure was fixed for the Monday of the ensuing week. On the Sunday the blind girl expressed a wish for the last time to visit the Prussian spring, a spot she had often visited with much pleasure before she lost her sight. Accordingly, the father and mother accompanied their child to the spring. Full of sad and anxious thoughts, they rested on the marble seat in the shade of those magnificent firs, when a sudden glad cry roused them from their reverie: "Father, mother, I can see!" How can one describe the feeling of deep gratitude with which these three happy people returned to Graefenberg and to their benefactor?

It was not only in moments of danger that Priessnitz showed his strength of mind. Each day, when prescribing for his patients, he gave the impression of an interesting personality. He had no special hour or place for seeing his patients. He prescribed at night and by day, out of doors or in his house, in the street, in the sick-room, at balls, at meals. Wherever he showed himself he was immediately surrounded by patients, or some attendants came who had either some report to make or orders to ask for. On these occasions he seldom entered into conversation, and was chary of words. Many complaints have been made on this subject. It is no doubt desirable to be explicit when prescribing ; with a little detailed explanation on his part many a mistake might have been avoided.

Priessnitz's crisis was an extra-functional effort of the internal organs to get rid of morbid matter. It was set in motion by a deliberate, methodical treatment developed and pursued by Vincent Priessnitz — termed by the scientific world, "Hydrotherapia"—which comprises all "natural" remedial means, but chiefly the regulated use externally of pure water, of fresh air, of skin frictions and kneadings, of clothing, and internally of simple diet, of pure water-drinking, of injections, all used in judicious conjunction with open air (preferably hillside walking) exercise, and open air rest.

Crisis, effected by the water-cure, assumes many forms, some of which I may mention : Efflorescence of the skin, scattered itching eruptions, feverishness, critical sweating of glutinous acid or fœtid matter, boils, nausea, vomiting, diarrhœa, vicarious discharge from the liver and kidneys, local eruptions, and several other minor disturbances of the body, which are difficult to enumerate, but can easily be detected by a skilful hydropathic practitioner.

Briefly stated, a series of abnormal symptoms constitutes an acute disease. These symptoms are due to a morbid condition of some of the organs of the body.

If the efforts employed to get rid of the derangement be only partially successful, the symptoms become more or less of a permanent character, and the disease is then termed chronic. Disease is curable when and just in so far as the system is or can be made sufficiently strong to eject all morbid matter, and to rebuild healthily the parts where the morbid matter rested ; but disease is incurable when any serious change of structure has taken place.

The aim of treatment should be to aid the development of the latent powers of the system to rid its organs of mischief. That mischief usually consists in the congestion or anæmia of some internal organ to the detriment of other parts of the body. The circulation of the blood is under the influence of the nervous system, whose power and efforts must be directed to strengthen and arouse the vascular structures to dissipate all morbid matter ; hence curative action is effected through the instrumentality of the nervous system. Violent and sudden stimulation of the nerves is followed by exhaustion, inflammation, and congestion ; but the gradual and judiciously regulated stimulation of the nervous system by hydropathic means conduces to the development and maintenance of its strength.

Organic life depends for its existence upon pure water, pure air, proper diet, regulated exercise and rest ; and these are the chief agents in effecting the cure of disease, inasmuch as they aid the normal efforts of the body through the instrumentality of the nerve force.

In the due apportionment of these agents, according to the powers of the constitution and the phases of disease as ascertained by medical examination, consists the scientific and the safe practice of the water-cure.

The result of hydropathic treatment is shown in one of the following ways :

1. The re-establishment of obstructed and suppressed secretions ;

2. The elimination of diseased matters through the bowels, kidneys, or skin ;

3. The formation of a critical action of some sort on the skin.

Such results constitute the crisis of the water-cure.

The crisis, being the result of the intrinsic efforts of the vital organs, is to be viewed as the signal of their relief.

A crisis being the evidence of cure of the internal disease, no recurrence of the latter is to be apprehended unless the morbid causes are reapplied.

It is, however, possible, and in a great number of cases it happens, that complete recovery from disease is effected by a slow process, without any perceptible evidence of a crisis, either external or internal.

The skilful manner in which Priessnitz applied his treatment so as to induce a crisis, and the medical intelligence exhibited in regulating his applications to each patient so as to achieve a successful issue, were unique. It is questionable whether there has ever been another man born possessing the same amount of insight and originality in dealing with human ailments.

Mr. John Greaves, of Leamington, published a reprint of the work by Sir John Floyer, M.D., and Dr. Baynard, in 1844, after having been restored to complete health, as a grateful acknowledgment of what hydropathic treatment had done for him. The following is an extract from the preface :

" In my seventieth year I was induced by the earnest recommendations of a much - esteemed friend, who had, during a residence of upwards of twelve months at Graefenberg, witnessed the wonderful power of the system, to place myself in the Prestbury Hydropathic Establishment, Cheshire.

" I was labouring under a serious affection of the heart, of long standing, great general debility, irregularity of all the secretions, dropsy in my legs, and fearful despondency. I was cased in flannel, and doomed to almost total inaction. Many were the warnings I received from medical advisers and friends against the application of the cold-water system ; but having already experienced the incompetency of medicine to arrest the progress of my disease, I resolved to judge for myself.

" On the 24th of October, eight days after having commenced the treatment, I was enabled to discontinue the use of flannel next the skin, where I had worn it for thirty years, my digestion was restored, and the whole character of my feelings was undergoing a change. It was now plain that those who had learnedly declaimed so much against hydropathy could have had no practical knowledge of its scientific application. The manner in which one part of the treatment followed another, without offering the slightest shock to my system, secured my confidence.

" In less than ten weeks the dropsy in the legs had entirely disappeared, a numbness only remaining which continued gradually to yield, and ultimately, on January 11, I was enabled to return home with a constitution renovated, the functions of the body regular, and my mind free from those depressed emotions under which it had so long laboured. What has been thus blessedly accomplished for me at Prestbury may likewise be effected for others, not at Prestbury only, but at any establishment where the air is equally salubrious, the water equally pure, and the system equally well administered. Nine months have now elapsed since I took leave of Prestbury, during which time I have continued to enjoy uninterrupted health of body and tranquillity of mind."

"The principle of scientific hydropathy—that is, the renewal of the body by water and food—the increase of growth secondary to the increase of moulting—is no quackery. It is not an underhand mode of doing nothing . . . but a *bonâ fide* use of a powerful agent."—SIR T. KING CHAMBERS, F.R.C.P., etc., "Renewal of Life," p. 369.

CHAPTER VIII

MEDICAL VIEWS AND PROCEDURE—*continued*

ONE powerful remedy which helped Priessnitz in his cures was the pure air of Graefenberg.

Fresh air is, like water, essential to the well-being of mankind, and the quality of the air lived in not only exercises an immediate effect on the process of respiration, but on the action of the blood, and influences considerably the mental disposition. Vitiated air weakens the nerves, interferes with the digestion, and encourages hypochondria, while pure air facilitates all the functions and makes folk light-hearted and cheerful. This was the reason why Priessnitz insisted so energetically on abundant fresh air for his patients. He advised them to be careful to ensure good ventilation in their dwellings in all seasons, night and day. If he found in a sick-room doors and windows closed, he mildly remonstrated, and, if necessary, he sharply reproved such injurious habits. He often opened a window himself to give access to the outer air. He was pleased when his patients spent the greater part of the day out of doors, and it was surprising to see the rapid progress those made who, during the water-cure, went out of doors as much as possible. To assure the complete success of a cure it is not only necessary to be out of doors, but to take a great deal of bodily exercise.*

Exercise is necessary to ensure warmth after a cold or tepid bath. Those who from various reasons were unable to move about sufficiently, had to split and saw wood, and were ordered gymnastic exercise.

When able to do so, patients were encouraged to take long walks in the early morning (during the summer months they started at 4 a.m.). A stranger would have been surprised to see Graefenberg at that time: everybody seemed to be about, and an active life reigned throughout the colony. It seemed, indeed, especially dedicated to the regeneration of poor ailing mankind. Mountain scenery, as a rule, makes a deeper impression on the hearts of men than a flat, monotonous

---

* Priessnitz did not approve of warm or heavy clothing for his patients. Nobody, even in winter, which is very severe at Graefenberg, was allowed to wear flannel under-clothing. People went about with their necks bare, and the men wore no ties, and only a few wore waistcoats. Plentiful exercise in the open air had to supply the necessary warmth.

country, and this is especially the case with Graefenberg. An indescribably poetic charm pervades
this lovely spot; the mountains are not rugged,
nor of excessive height, and beautiful pine-woods
cover them up to their summit. And these woods
—how cool and balmy!* How richly peopled
with legends of past centuries! How soothing to
body and mind to dwell amongst their shade,
never to be forgotten by those who have once
been there! Nor must the delicious water of the
Graefenberg springs be ignored. In other countries the tired wanderer often sighs for the clear
water of a mountain stream to assuage his thirst
and refresh his weary limbs. Not so at Graefenberg. Here every hundred yards the bountiful
earth sends the most delicious water forth for your
refreshment unstintingly.

Priessnitz prescribed for the benefit of his
patients a simple and nourishing diet of vegetable
and animal food.

Scientific men are generally agreed that the
higher animals, and especially man, require for
their food varied kinds of nourishment.

By experience Priessnitz arrived at the same
conclusions. For breakfast he ordered milk and
bread-and-butter, which contain most of the neces-

---

* The Graefenberg forests are the property of the Archi-
episcopal See of Breslau, with free and unlimited access for
the public.

sary ingredients. Milk alone, being composed of sugar and the component parts of butter and cheese, contains sufficient nourishment in itself to be a universal food. The aromatic wood straw-berries, which are gathered in quantities in the pine-forests from the middle of May to the middle of October, form an indispensable item of the Graefenberg breakfast, to which are added honey and fresh eggs.

According to his arrangement, the dinner at Graefenberg consisted generally of one course of meat and vegetables, and of one course of what in this country would be called a milk-pudding. On Fridays was added to this a course of trout, and on Sundays a second course of meat. The bread was the ordinary mixed household bread, made of coarse rye flour, mixed with a little leaven of groats.*

He used to say : "The groat leaven in the bread is the same for the human body as the little stones are for poultry, and the sand-grains for birds."

Together with an otherwise well-regulated diet, this bread proves to be very beneficial to patients suffering from troubles of the bowels, and it cured young Prince Lichtenstein entirely of chronic constipation. This prince derived the greatest advantage from the diet prescribed for him by

* Latterly the excellent Graham bread has taken its place.

III

Priessnitz, as well as from the cold-water treatment in general.

Some patients took their food nearly, others quite, cold. Priessnitz made an observation which a century earlier the celebrated Hahn had made before him. Animals whose intestines resemble closely those of the human body, when fed with warm fodder, become weak and tender. He had therefore a great objection to anything being taken hot, and soup was banished altogether from the Graefenberg dinner-table.

During cold-water treatment, as we have already remarked, the entire organism is in a heightened state of activity. The process of secretion is accelerated, as well as the circulation of the blood to the capillaries, and the natural result is the sensation of increased appetite.*

---

* When hydropathy was first introduced into England, a similar diet was observed with the same excellent results, although the food was perhaps a trifle less rough, and better prepared. People have complained that Priessnitz paid little attention to the *quality* of the food, insisting especially on the *quantity* consumed. As far as my opinion is concerned, I rather endorse the plan of quantity *versus* quality. The fact of the heightened state of activity of the whole organism during the water-cure makes it of primary importance that the waste of the body should not exceed the supply ; so, judging from his great success, it seems evident that Priessnitz's view on the subject was correct. In most hydropathic establishments on the Continent the same strict rules as to diet are observed, whilst in England, I am sorry to say, many of our so-called hydros are really hotels and boarding-

The gigantic appetite of his patients, the wish on Priessnitz's part to allow them fully to satisfy it, and finally the colossal provision therefor in the kitchen, made meals at Graefenberg a curious and unique spectacle.

The large dining-hall contained three, four, and, during the summer season, five large tables. Between three and four hundred persons of both sexes, of all ages, classes, and nations, assembled there at meal-time (2 p.m.). Soon after the first bell they began to drop in. To fill up the time till dinner was served, some played battledore and shuttlecock, laughing and shouting; others ran up and down the hall to get warm after their cold sitz-baths. Some exercised their mental digestion by reading bits from the daily papers of all nations, which covered a large round table, while others conversed in tones which, amidst the hubbub, were not of the softest.*

Soon after the second bell appeared the waitresses with the dishes. They were welcomed by the hungry crowd, and as each hastened to his or her own place at table, the huge hall was for

---

houses, providing elaborate *menus* with every imaginable delicacy.—R. M.

* John Gibbs, " Letters from Graefenberg ": At dinner were between two and three hundred persons of all ages and all ranks who, with perhaps a dozen exceptions, were invalids, a circumstance which no one unacquainted with the fact would have suspected.

a few moments the scene of much activity. Once arrived at their destination, only one idea took possession of each individual. All conventionality was forgotten, the exigencies of polite society were, so to say, buried in oblivion, and man's primitive condition, only bent on satisfying hunger, triumphed for a short time over all other considerations. The simple costermonger entirely ignored his neighbour, the ex-Minister of State, and the fiery Southerner seemed unaware of having at his side a lovely and delicate daughter of Albion. Hunger, the autocrat, reigned supreme, and everyone was bent on paying homage to the mighty sovereign.*

Priessnitz enjoyed seeing his patients eat as much as possible—yea, even more than enough sometimes. Dr. Selinger, who on this point did not share his friend's ideas, and did not approve of the ways of some of the visitors, ventured to remark on it occasionally. But Priessnitz always took the hungry patients' part, and could never be made to see that over-eating could do harm while under the water-cure.

* R. T. Claridge, Esq.: "I can testify that what I saw at the dinner-table at Graefenberg surpassed all my expectations, for everybody ate with such appetites and in such quantities that, but for my conviction of being amongst invalids labouring under all kinds of diseases (most of which were thought incurable by the most celebrated and clever of the faculty), I should have thought they were a number of workmen, perfectly robust and healthy."

The cold-water cure makes great demands on the patient's energy and perseverance, and imposes on him much self-denial and self-control. It is interesting to note how differently persons of different nationalities, of different sex and classes of society, behaved during the treatment. After many years' experience and observation, Priessnitz made the following remarks on this subject :

The least energy and perseverance is shown by Israelites and Russians. Next come Danes and Swedes, while greater endurance is shown by Germans and Magyars. After these follow Spaniards, Italians, Americans, English, French, and Poles.

In general, patients from southern climates make quicker and more thorough cures than patients from cold countries. Once the fear of cold water is overcome, women are more persevering and courageous than men. The clergy lose the necessary courage soonest ; men belonging to the military profession latest.

The greatest opposition to the water-cure is found amongst the middle classes and poor people. The well-to-do tradesman despises it as being cheap, and therefore worthless. The poor man is suspicious, fearing that water instead of medicine is prescribed in order to save the expense. But the praise of many thousand persons who have

regained their health at Graefenberg has resounded in all parts of the globe.

In the eleven years 1831 - 1841 over 7,219
strangers visited Graefenberg for the water-cure.
A majority of these cases were considered very
bad or hopeless by their medical attendants, and
yet only thirty-eight deaths occurred amongst
them, the average age at death being over forty
years, and most of these cases were of an utterly
hopeless nature on their arrival at Graefenberg,
where they insisted on remaining, when Priessnitz
unwillingly acceded to their entreaties to try and
relieve some of the symptoms.*

* James Wilson, " The Water-Cure," 4th edition, London,
1842. Condensed from pp. 30-32.

THE TREATMENT.

(1) V. Priessnitz. (2) Dr. Schindler.

(3) Dripping-sheet.

(4) Air-bath.

(5) Water-drinking.

(6) Dew-bath.

(7) The Pack.

(8) Taking out of Pack.

(9) Cold plunge-bath.

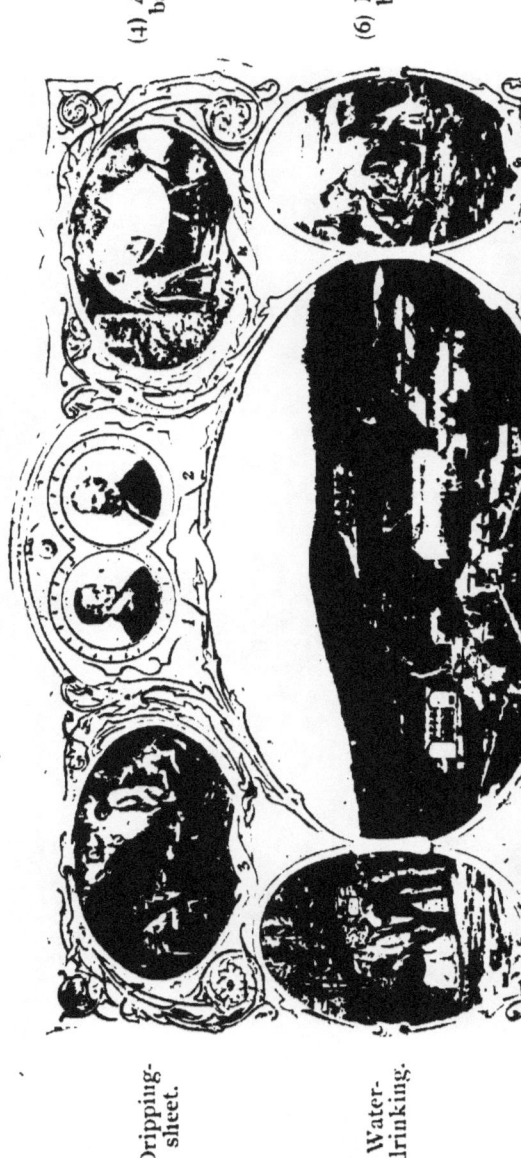

GRÆFENBERG.

To face p. 116.

CHAPTER IX

Colonel Ripper's Letter

IN this chapter I give a full translation of Colonel Ripper's famous "open missive letter," which has now passed through nearly fifty editions. It contains a complete and interesting account of Priessnitz's mode of treatment, and of the applications as used by him.

This document is of special interest, as it shows that the hydropathist, Father Kneipp, from whose great work in aid of suffering humanity we have no wish to detract, is not, as he has been called, a new health apostle, but an able and enthusiastic follower of his great predecessor, Vincent Priessnitz, whose work he took up where Priessnitz left it. Father Kneipp has chosen to invest old well-known appliances, which he uses with new names. The obscure "little book," which revealed to him the excellency of the water treatment, and by means of which he saved his own life, as he tells us himself, was, no doubt, one of the many pamphlets or handbooks on the subject which appeared during Priessnitz's lifetime. Hydropathy had been introduced into this country, and the appliances which Father Kneipp claims as his own invention were in use in the United Kingdom where the hydropathic system was carried out in its entirety before Father Kneipp was heard of.

The *herb-cure* which Father Kneipp includes in his "new treatment" had also been practised with a certain amount of success, as I ascertained during my recent visit to Graefenberg, curiously enough in that same district, by a man of humble birth, a contemporary of Vincent Priessnitz.

" [*Forty-third Edition.*]

" *Open Missive Letter to Father Kneipp by Colonel Ripper.*

" GRAEFENBERG,
" *September*, 1893.

" Nothing is further from me in writing these lines than any feeling of animosity ; on the contrary, as son-in-law of Vincent Priessnitz, I feel grateful to you for having given a fresh impulse to hydropathy, and I fully recognise your merit in having achieved so many successful cures.

" But nevertheless I owe it to the memory of my father-in-law, whose whole life, from his earliest manhood, was devoted to the interest of suffering humanity, to address you the following lines. Not only myself, but a great number of admirers and friends of the method of healing by water, which is solely based on the laws of Nature, have been painfully impressed by the fact of your omitting to mention, even by a word, in any of the twenty-two editions of your work, ' My Water-Cure,' the founder and inventor of the water-cure, Vincent Priessnitz.*

"The recognition by you of the merits of the Father of Hydropathy would not have diminished your own fame in any way; on the contrary, it would have enhanced it.

"I do not for a moment entertain the idea that you wish to be looked upon as the messenger of a new gospel of healing, although you so carefully avoid mentioning in any way Priessnitz and his method of curing with water. By ignoring your great and far-famed predecessor, you do not, believe me, reverend sir, add to your own greatness. The cause of hydropathy and its adherents would have been much furthered if you had contented yourself with adding to the fair edifice as you found it. People expected that at least you would have shown sufficient courtesy to the memory of Priessnitz to mention his name honourably in the lectures

---

* Having carefully read this book, which is perhaps not generally known in England, I corroborate the above statement.

you gave in Austria, whose son he is, a son of whom his country has a right to be justly proud. You preferred, however, not to do so. When, in your twenty-eighth year, you were struck down with sickness, so serious as to be given up by the doctors, a booklet fell into your hands, as you state on page 2 of your work, 'quite accidentally,' in the year 1848, which treated of the water-cure, and through which, after studying it, you entirely cured yourself.*

"As the work named is rather voluminous, containing 290 pages, and therefore cannot be called a 'small unsightly booklet,' I herewith, in the interest of historical truth and justice, ask you to name the book and its real title. Might it not rather have been one of the numerous booklets or pamphlets which appeared before 1848 on Priessnitz and his method of healing in Germany, and especially in Bavaria and elsewhere?

"Priessnitz, like yourself, cured himself when given up by the doctors, with the only difference that he had no *book* on the water-cure to help him, but only his own great and powerful mind, which inspired him to read the *book of Nature*, and therefrom to learn and understand the truth.

---

* Some people thought this book had been a work by Dr. J. S. Hahn : " Instructions on the Power and Effect of Cold Water," published at Breslau and Leipzig by Daniel Pietsch, 1749, in the German language.

COLONEL RIPPER'S LETTER

"Only through his own exertions, not suddenly, only by degrees, and through continued experiments, Priessnitz acquired his knowledge of the different ways of applying cold water. In the beginning of his career he used a sponge, with which he bathed the parts injured by contusions, or otherwise wounded, applying also compresses.

"Later on, when sought by people suffering from gout, he let them perspire, covered with feather beds, and after that he gave them first tepid and then cold baths, in a big washtub, letting them be well rubbed whilst in the bath.

"Mr. T. Knur, from Kuchelnau, near Ratibor in Prussian Silesia, a gentleman in the employ of Prince Lichnowski, wrote, in 1830, a detailed account of this matter to Professor Oertel, of Anspach, who quotes it in his work in German, 'The Latest Water-Cures' (Part III., page 17, published by F. Campe, Nuremberg, 1830).

"In consequence of complaints made by a local doctor, the suspected sponge and some of the Graefenberg water were chemically analyzed in the presence of the Freiwaldau magistrates. Nothing unusual was discovered either in water or sponge; nevertheless Priessnitz was forbidden the use of the latter. From that time forward Priessnitz only used the flat hand to rub his patients, and was even more successful than before, as now 'life came upon life,' or 'flesh upon flesh,' as he quaintly expressed himself.

"In order not to make the patient's skin sore with protracted rubbing, Priessnitz had a linen sheet, wrung out more or less dry, wrapped round the patient, either in a sitting or reclining position. Out of this proceeding evolved eventually the very efficient and frequently used friction with a wet-sheet ('abreibung'), the slapping with the wet-sheet ('abklatschen'), and stripping off the wet-sheet ('abstreifen'). Later on Priessnitz ordered some patients to be wrapped in blankets and well covered over with feather beds, to promote perspiration by a dry process. Previous to the wrapping in blankets, the suffering parts of the patient's body were covered with a wet compress in order to stimulate the action of the skin on the inert and suffering limbs, which, after some time, always proved successful.

"One of the patients, who, with the exception of his head, which in consequence of congestions was in a permanent state of perspiration, could not be got to perspire, although covered with numerous blankets and feather beds, gave Priessnitz the idea to try what might be called a compress on a large scale, and to obtain for the entire body the same result as had partially been achieved with the compress.

"He ordered the patient to be wrapped entirely,

with the exception of the head, in a well-wrung-out wet sheet, the blanket and the bedding to be arranged as usual afterwards. While in this pack the patient's head, which was hot and perspiring, was bathed constantly with cold water. After some time of this treatment Priessnitz succeeded in getting this patient into regular perspirations, which resulted by degrees in a complete cure. The outcome of this experience was the perspiring in wet-sheets, and what is known as the pack.*

"Owing to mistakes and disobedience on the part of some patients, Priessnitz discovered many different hydropathic appliances; but solely by *his own observations* and *keen insight* did he come to these conclusions, the outcome of which were: The head-bath, the cold full bath, the tepid,

---

* Drs. James Wilson and Manby Gully (father of the present Speaker of the House of Commons), in their interesting book, "The Practice of the Water-Cure," published at Malvern in 1846, call the pack "the crowning discovery of the water-cure"; and, further, "Whatever additional discoveries may be made, or improvements introduced into the practice of the water-cure, Priessnitz will always deserve the credit of having established and put together a system of treatment which, when contemplated by the physiological eye, is beautiful in its power, efficacy, and simplicity, but whose value can only be appreciated to its fullest extent by those who understand and have made the human body their study, and at the same time are enabled to compare it with the results of medicinal treatment by having practised both."

shallow, sitz, eye, foot, leg, arm, elbow, hand, mouth, nose, sole, dew, air-water,* sun, and alternating baths; the half-bath, the douches, as well as various kinds of compresses, such as (*a*) The damp anti-inflammatory; (*b*) the soothing, warming; (*c*) the warmth-producing compress; the abdominal, eye, cross bandages; the compress on the calf of the leg, and on other parts of the body. Furthermore, various injections, and also that most useful and beneficial rubbing in and after the bath.

" As mentioned already, Priessnitz invented the sweating, not only in dry blankets, but also in wet-sheets, also the slight perspiration to warm the body up. Furthermore, the half and three-quarter packs, which only leave the arms free, the trunk pack, and for nervous and delicate persons the beneficent and shallow tepid bath immediately after getting out of bed. He ordered in some cases sponging of the whole body, and of separate parts; the pouring over of cold water; enemas; the temporary wearing of wet shirts by night and by day, and in certain cases patients had to go bareheaded and barefooted. His principle was to strengthen the body, in order to enable it to eject noxious matters. He recognised also the existence of purely nervous diseases.

* With open windows, to obtain plentiful access of oxygen.

"Another rule of his was to use in acute diseases only *tepid*, never cold, water, with the exception of a few, amongst which was cholera.

"Special care was bestowed on people with an impaired circulation, which he endeavoured to restore to a normal state by means based on the laws of Nature. He ordered those patients a strong or a mild nourishing diet. Some dyspeptic patients were put on an entirely cold diet. A separate table with suitable and easily-digested food was kept for them. Some patients received a strong, some a mild, treatment only *once* a day.*

"He disapproved of alcoholic drinks, and ordered patients who were unable to digest milk to drink *coffee* made of *corn*.

"In some cases, especially gout and syphilis, he forbade animal food, and to those suffering from abdominal disorders he ordered coarse black rye bread.

"One of his principal rules was never to order a bath without ascertaining that the patient's

* The usual number of treatments at Graefenberg in Priessnitz's time was three : the first took place early in the morning, the second about eleven o'clock a.m., and the third in the course of the afternoon. Treatment, however, as has been shown in several cases, especially in the one of his own daughter Sophie, and which must appear severe in the extreme to the ordinary mind, differed very much, according to the requirements of each individual patient.—R. M.

body contained sufficient warmth to produce a thorough reaction. For the same reason, he never allowed one bath to follow another before the reaction produced by the first bath had fully taken place.

" His healing agents were water, suitable diet, and out - of - door exercise. He once said to Kalliwoda, Prior of the convent Raigern in Moravia : 'If I had no water, I should cure with air alone.'*

"And may I ask who was the first to open windows in sick-rooms, and to order patients fresh air day and night ? Who else but the peasant boy, Vincent Priessnitz, who through numberless marvellous cures obtained the fame which is actually his, to whom the gratitude of thousands of people of every nation, restored by him to health and well-being, has erected on the Graefenberg those splendid monuments in stone and bronze which bear witness to his greatness.

" He was the inventor of the anti-inflammatory, vivifying, strengthening, calming, and tone-giving treatment, and of the fundamental principle of

---

* Dr. James Wilson says, in his " Practice of the Water-Cure ": " Priessnitz, after an experience of twenty-five years, considers the quality of the air and water of more consequence than the shape, colour, and material of the bath, or the size and comfort of the rooms. There is no reason, however, why the patient should not have large, airy rooms, and every rational English comfort."

hydriation, namely, *that the cold bath is only refresh-ing and beneficial when the skin is warm or per-spiring.*

" Every word I have written here is the absolute truth, and I am prepared to give the proofs of it if necessary. I have at my disposal a whole literature of hydropathy, of more than one hundred volumes, nearly all on Priessnitz and his work. Amongst them one, in German, by Dr. Schnitzlein, called ' Observations and Experiments to establish the Water-Cure ' (published by G. Franz, Munich). The author stayed at Graefenberg in 1837, as well as Professor Hamer in 1838, both sent by the Bavarian Government. The celebrated hydro-path, Dr. Oertel, of Anspach, did not mind the trouble of a long journey to Graefenberg, at a time when there were no railways, in order to gather information from Priessnitz himself; whereas you, reverend sir, did not think it worth your while during your recent stay at Neisse, a town situated only one and a half hours by rail from Graefenberg, to visit a spot which is justly called the cradle of hydropathy, and where its noble founder has found his last resting-place.

" You replied to the gentleman who suggested this visit to you : ' I have my own Woerishofen !' I can assure you that you would have found much to interest you at Graefenberg which has never reached the ears of the general public, and which, in spite of Woerishofen, would have amply repaid you for the small trouble. You might have shown more respect to Graefenberg and its immortal master, as your fundamental principles and the whole of your water-cure, only under different names, are taken from Priessnitz. Where ideas and principles are identical, different appellations and modifications are of little importance.

" Your ' Spanish cloak ' is nothing else but the ' pack ' (also called ' wickel ') invented by Priessnitz.

" Your ' unterwickel,' the three-quarter or half-pack.

" Your 'short wickel,' the trunk pack.

" Your ' water -jet,' mild, partial douches in ordinary use at Graefenberg.

"Your ' lightning jet,' the great douche with concentrated jet.

" Your ' water-walking or treading,' the leg and sole baths.

" Even the ' not drying ' after any of the water-treatments which you so much recommend, and which is looked upon as something quite new in hydropathy, has been practised by Professor Oertel himself, according to his work, ' The Newest Water-Cures ' (page 27), as early as the year 1830. (He ordered patients to be put to bed without having been dried previously.)

" Priessnitz himself ordered patients suffering

from throat complaints, when out walking, to wash their throat and back of neck at the springs, and to continue their walk, and let the water evaporate without drying it with a towel.

"Priessnitz left a new system of healing based on the laws of Nature, and which is therefore true and scientific, and which has been recognised by numerous qualified doctors as such. You tell the world nothing *new* in your book, but I think it is a great and noble act, reverend sir, that you, a respected and influential man, have done in leading erring mankind back into the right path, which had been, before you, trodden by Vincent Priessnitz.

"The heartiest thanks are, however, due to all the hydropaths of Germany who, under great difficulties, have not only enabled hydropathy to hold its own, but have done so much to spread it over this country.

"I remain, reverend sir,

"Respectfully and obediently yours,

"HANS RIPPER."

Father Kneipp died on June 17, 1897, at the age of seventy-six, at Woerishofen in Bavaria. He was born at Stephanried, May 17, 1821. He took orders in 1852, and in 1881 was placed in charge of the parish of Woerishofen, where he laboured up to the time of his death in the dual capacity of pastor of souls and healer of bodies. Although but little can be added to Colonel Ripper's exhaustive letter on Father Kneipp's system, we feel that some words of acknowledgment are due to a man who has so largely, and, we must add, so disinterestedly, contributed to the well-being of a great number of his contemporaries.

Professor Herkomer, R.A., in his interesting appreciation of Father Kneipp in the *Daily Graphic*, London, June 18, 1897, says: " In reading over his book, I cannot find much that is original in Herr Kneipp's use of water : that was all done by the inventor, the inspired peasant Priessnitz, and it may have been Herr Kneipp's good fortune to find a copy of this man's book in that royal library, as I fancy that book has long been rare."

The query as to where Father Kneipp got his information from is simply in a nutshell. There is no doubt whatever that the treatise referred to was an account of Priessnitz's work at Graefenberg. This fact is borne out by the description of appliances given in Herr Kneipp's book entitled, " My Water-Cure," being the same even in details as those used by Priessnitz. Between the years 1833 and 1848 there was a very large number of books and pamphlets published ; a list of many of them is given in a subsequent chapter.

Owing to the perusal of one of these pamphlets (accidentally discovered) discoursing upon the powerful curative effects of water appliances, Father Kneipp resolved to try the treatment. It appears that when a young man he was very delicate and predisposed to contract consumption; and to make a long story short, we are informed that he cured himself. It is well to note here that the starting-point of both Vincent Priessnitz's and Father Kneipp's career was from practical experience of the water-treatment on their own bodies, prescribed without having had any previous medical training; and apart from the slight difference between these two men's modes of treatment, they gained for themselves a wider reputation in the field of hydrotherapeutics than any other two medical men have ever done.

Between the years 1848 and 1881 hundreds of books were published that spread the fame of Priessnitz all over the world; but until Father Kneipp took charge of the parish of Woerishofen, in 1881, he (Kneipp) had never been heard of.

Father Kneipp's real and great merit was in his firm and enthusiastic belief in a natural and simple mode of life for everybody, whether in good or in bad health. Furthermore, being convinced of the curative power of water, air and sunshine, he succeeded by the systematic carrying into practice of his principles, by great energy, and with much skill, to restore thousands of persons of every class of society to health and strength, impressing upon

the world at large the great truth that man, if he
wishes to enjoy health of mind and body, must
observe the laws of Nature, and obey her teachings
conscientiously throughout his natural life. Father
Kneipp also had great faith in the efficacy of
herbs, and in his book the description of his remedies and medicinal preparations is most quaint
and reminiscent of the times and customs of the
Middle Ages, all his applications being directed,
as he says, "towards purifying the blood and
saps." Botanical medicines are far from obsolete,
for we see with interest that Dr. Fernie's book,
" Herbal Simples Approved for Modern Use of
Cure,"* has reached its second edition.

* W. T. Fernie, " Herbal Simples." John Bright and Co.,
Bristol, 1895 ; 2nd edition, 1897, pp. xxiv., 652.

CHAPTER X

GRAEFENBERG AND ITS CURE

ON my visit to Graefenberg in the autumn of 1895, I was struck by the beauty of its scenery, as well as by its favourable meteorological conditions.

The fine forest (principally of pine-trees) in close proximity to the establishments, and the world-famed "spring territory," cover nearly thirty English square miles, and are provided with well-kept and extensive roads. The fragrant odour of these gigantic pines constitutes, so to say, a natural inhalatorium.

He who will add to his pleasant experiences, let him go and visit one morning in early summer or autumn the Graefenberg woods and their springs.* Let him take a refreshing draught at the House Spring before starting, then go to the

* Nearly all the fountains at Graefenberg were erected to the memory of Priessnitz—many before his death, and several since.

pine-wood close by, and, passing the Marien-Joseph and Ferdinand Springs, seek to reach the Priessnitz Spring, which boasts of the best water, finally choosing the Bernstein, with its lovely view, as his goal. He will find frequent opportunity to refresh himself on his way to that rugged peak at the Ladies', the Gold, the Louisa, the Vienna, and the Ice Springs. Or he may pursue the steep path leading to the Bohemian Spring, and· from there to the Hirschkamm. After having tasted the crystal water of the last-named spring, and thereby gathered new strength, he may extend his walk to the Spring of Friendship, to the German Spring—the highest in altitude of all the springs, with its mighty water-jet—and from there proceed to the rock called " Oswald's Joy." On that mountain he will be rewarded for his exertion by a magnificent panorama. Not to be forgotten are the Sophien Spring and the lovely Prussian and Pine Springs. From that point the road leads to the Hirschbad Spring, the Springs of Good Hope, and the Jäger Spring. On his way back to Graefenberg the wanderer will wend his way through majestic pine-woods, passing the Styrian and Finnish Springs, the Diamond and Vincent Springs, and his whole being will be refreshed ; he will feel the blood coursing through his veins with new vigour ; he will realize that his hope of renewed health is not a vain fancy ;

his heart will be filled with gratitude, and his soul with joy.

The excellent roadway ascending from Freiwaldau to Graefenberg, about a mile's distance, was built in 1846 by several grateful inhabitants of Hamburg cured by Priessnitz, and thus it derives its name of " Hamburger Steg " (Hamburg Path).

A few minutes' walk brings the pedestrian to a shelter with the cheery words, "Glueck auf" (Good luck to you)! From this point the eye embraces the sunny Biele valley, with the villages of Buchelsdorf, Adelsdorf, Thomasdorf, and Waldenburg. To the south-west rises the stately mountain-range of the Altvater, which forms part of the Sudeten mountains. To the south-east rise the Bielekamm (Biele Ridge) and the Goldkamm, which derived its name from gold-mines which were worked for several centuries, but which are now abandoned. To the west lies the Staritz Valley, with the villages of Nieder-Lindewiese, the seat of the well-known " Schroth " establishment, and to the east lie Freiwaldau, Boehmischdorf, and several other hamlets.

The next resting-place on this charming road is " Gilbert Stone," with the words—full of meaning — " You must be patient," addressed by Priessnitz in 1844 to Mr. Thomas Marley Gilbert, one of his English patients—we dare say only one of many to whom this advice was given. Here one gets the first glimpse of "the colony," the oldest part of Graefenberg. The path now winds for a short time through rich pasture-land, and soon the attention is arrested by the "French Monument," a stately fountain in the shape of a granite pyramid bearing the inscription, "Au génie de l'eau froide," erected by the grateful French.

On entering Graefenberg proper, we pass a building devoted to public amusements, which boasts of a splendid kegelbahn (bowling-green)—a popular game amongst the Germans.

Facing the band-stand, at the further end of the public promenade, is the famous Bohemian monument representing Hygeia on a marble pyramid, the pedestal base showing on one side a portrait in high relief of Priessnitz, and the other side bearing an inscription in the Bohemian language, which translated into English is :

"Water above all !

"To water we owe our being, growth, and health, and what Thales of yore foresaw dimly, Priessnitz has triumphantly brought to light."

From this point a delightful and extensive panorama lies before the spectator's eye, embracing the country for many miles around far into the fertile plains of Prussian Silesia.

On turning to the right, the road leads to the so-called "Priessnitz Koppe," a gentle elevation,

Principal Monuments & Springs

SOPHIA SPRING

PRIESSNITZ SPRING

MECKLENBURGH SPRING

FRENCH SPRING

PRIESSNITZ MAUSOLEUM

BOHEMIAN SPRING

HUNGARIAN MONUMENT

POLISH SPRING

PRUSSIAN SPRING

ENGLISH SPRING

MUSIC PAVILION

To face p. 136.

one of the loveliest spots in this beautiful place, and a favourite walk with the Graefenberg visitors, because in some parts it is sheltered almost entirely from wind. Many an enthusiastic admirer of Nature has extolled the beauties of this favoured spot, and the well-known author, Heinrich Laube, who, fifty years ago, sought and found health under Priessnitz's care, has awarded it a special chapter in his " Travelling Sketches."

In walking round the " Koppe," one comes to the " Mausoleum," a chapel, in the crypt of which Priessnitz and his wife are placed.

On the lonely footpath on the mountain-side overlooking Freiwaldau stands on a pedestal of granite a majestic bronze lion, the work of the sculptor Schwanthaler. It was erected in 1839, a gift of grateful Hungarians, and bears an appropriate inscription.

In the pine-wood, through which lies the path to the douches, rises over a clear mountain spring a fine marble monument, the gift of Prussian visitors, bearing the inscription in letters of gold, " To the immortal Priessnitz—The grateful Prussians."

On the Philosophen Steg (Philosopher's Path) stands the finest of all the monuments, the " King Carol Quelle " (King Charles's Spring), a gift of King Charles of Roumania, erected by him in the year 1888.

We might fill pages with the enumeration of many more of these springs, and extol the merits of the delicious quality of their water; we might enlarge on the description of the innumerable lovely walks and well-kept roads leading from one charming view to another. But we are afraid to exhaust our reader's patience, and will only add that the average temperature of the totality of springs, forty-four in number, ranges from 37° to 45° Fahr., and that the "Hausquelle" (House Spring), which draws its fine water partly from the Vincent Spring (named after Priessnitz's only son), and the Bohemian Spring, was a joint gift of all the patients and visitors assembled during one season to their benefactor Priessnitz.

The climate of Graefenberg is temperate, the winds being mostly westerly and southerly, and the thermometer very rarely rises above 76° Fahr.

The daily mean summer temperature is about 55° Fahr.; the average temperature of the whole year about 43° Fahr. The ozone contained in the air equals 8·7, Linder's scale.

The soil on the entire Graefenberg territory is gravel, which renders outdoor exercise possible even after heavy rainfalls.

Notwithstanding these favourable climatic conditions, there are, even in summer, many days of inclement weather, while in winter, which Priessnitz considered the best time for the cure of chronic

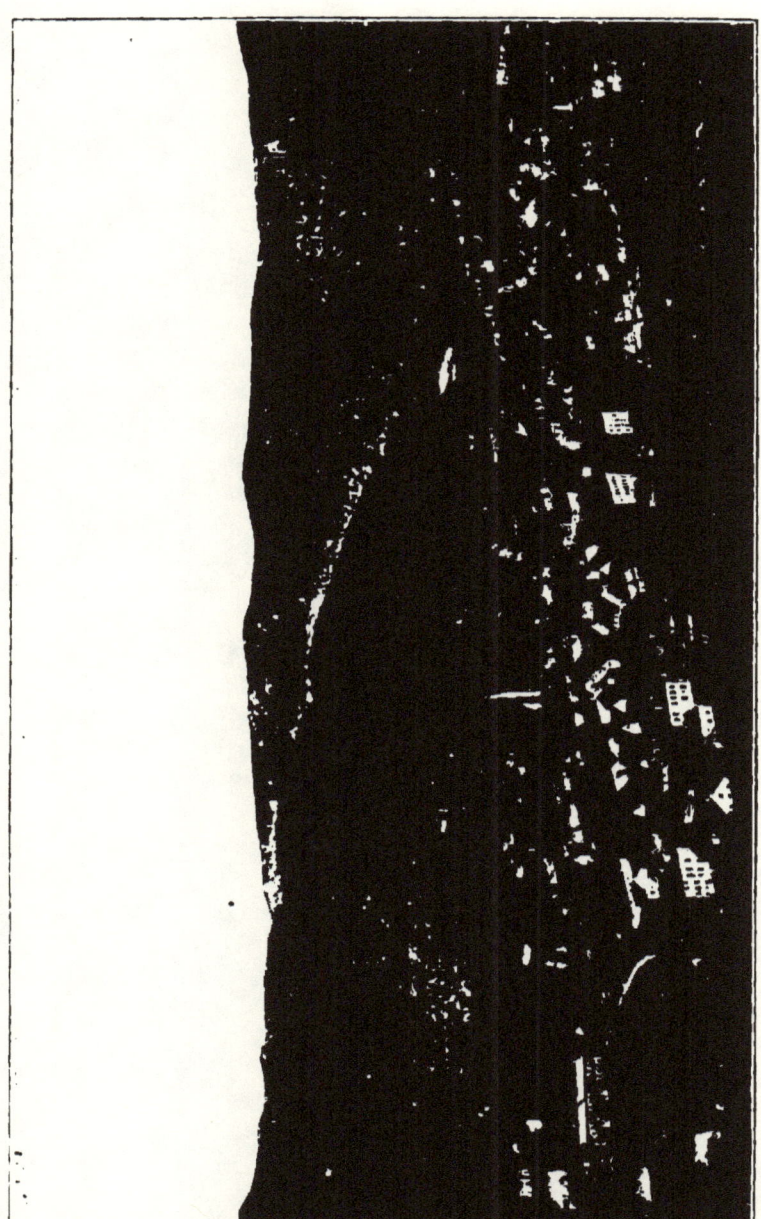

FREIWALDAU.

complaints,* those days occasionally extend to weeks; the daily exercise in the open air, so necessary in hydropathic treatment, being thus frequently interrupted. It seems to me that the Graefenberg authorities have not advanced as other health resorts have done, in meeting the general wants of the invalid population.

A covered way, or winter-garden, affording sufficient protection against the weather, would meet this difficulty in a satisfactory manner.

Priessnitz's favourite sudorific for inducing perspiration was natural exercise, but he found that it was neither sufficient nor even practicable in many cases of delicate people, and so he had frequent recourse to the tedious artificial sweating process of the blanket-pack, which was the only artificial sweating process employed by Priessnitz.

As a matter of course, medical science should move on in the same ratio as other sciences do;

---

* It must be borne in mind that much depends upon the waste and repair of the whole system. Priessnitz meant that patients suffering from chronic ailments, who are able to bear the cold, stand a better chance of complete cure during the winter, because the keen air acts as a strong tonic, whereas the heat of summer tends rather to enervate the system and thereby to diminish its power of recuperation. Priessnitz did not include in this class of patients those who, with no organic disease, suffer from a greater or lesser degree of chronic debility. In these cases he considered that the treatment was attended with better results in milder weather. From my own practice of more that forty years, I have been led to confirm and to entirely agree with these views.

thus the followers of Priessnitz have made some important additions to hydropathy in respect to the sudorifics by the introduction of the hot-air bath, etc.; by these additions the crises have been considerably modified in their severity all round.

Though now for the most part superseded as a general sudorific, the blanket-pack is still capable of doing good service in special cases. These are, for instance, sluggish or phlegmatic constitutions, in which the circulation has been for years in a state of torpor, with such symptoms as icy-cold extremities, blue and purple skin, chilblains, with slight œdema, languid circulation and inaction of the liver, kidneys and bowels, a condition of body which is unfavourably acted upon by high temperature prematurely applied. A more gradual sweating process is required in such cases, and the blanket "tuck-up," with hot bottles, etc., being the most convenient, and being attended with no risk, may be resorted to with advantage. It retains about the body its own heat by a process of gradual accumulation, so avoiding the risk attendant upon a sudden and powerful stimulation.

As an eliminator of morbific matter, however, the blanket has serious defects. In the first place, its comparatively low temperature renders its action feeble, and when the secretions have been brought to the surface they are, by being so long in close contact with the skin, liable to pass and repass through the skin as through a mucous membrane; the enhanced activity of the circulation accelerating this physiological action.

In the second place, the patient is compelled to breathe offensive exhalations escaping from the upper part of the envelope; and thirdly, eruptions are apt to be formed on the skin through the long-continued irritation. These defects greatly detract from the value of the blanket-pack, and I accordingly prefer confining its functions to those of a mild " heatent," preparatory to cool or cold applications, except in the cases already specified.

The lamp - bath has for its chief merit the expeditious character of the process, which is got through in from twenty to thirty minutes, instead of occupying, like the blanket-pack, from three to four hours. It is, besides, easily modified in a variety of ways to meet the several conditions subjected to its influence. It has its drawbacks, however. The space included for the heated air, whether by box, blanket, or mackintosh, is small, and soon becomes filled with noxious elements from the person, as well as from the process of combustion. The heat rises to the upper part of the body, and the air is more or less burnt to support the flame; and as it would thus be intolerable to the lungs, it cannot be grateful to what is, in point of fact, another lung—the skin.

The vapour - bath is eminently soothing and

agreeable to the skin, and in some diseases of that organ is preferable to any other sweating process. In point of speed it is even more convenient than the lamp-bath, producing sufficient perspiration in ten or fifteen minutes. It requires, however, to be managed with caution, as when overheated it unduly excites the action of the heart, and relaxes the skin by too much soddening.

Over all these " minor sudorifics " the Turkish hot-air bath possesses a very marked superiority. It is free from the objections of tediousness, unequal action of heat, noxious atmosphere, and relaxing moisture. It has been called "the short way to the water-cure," and, looking to results, not without reason. Under the stimulus of the heated oxygen, the system is roused to action, the circulation is accelerated, and the exhalation from skin and lung increased. There is a physiological tumult in which every organ has its action quickened, and the large amount of pure heated oxygen drawn into the system by the lungs and skin greatly aids in the decomposition of carbon, the augmentation of waste, and the elimination of foreign matter. While the effete and unhealthy elements are loosened by other hydropathic measures, the hot-air bath sweeps them away out of the circulation, as it is set in motion, through the skin, kidneys, and bowels; hence the old Graefenberg crisis is now anticipated during the course of treatment.

Had Priessnitz lived longer, I have no doubt that he would have added to his wonderful and extensive system the beneficent and invaluable appliance of hot-air rooms, so common now in hydropathic establishments, and generally known as Turkish baths. His keen and far-seeing mind would have grasped the incalculable advantage of this powerful adjunct to hydropathy.

The advantage of the hot-air bath is not unfrequently exhibited to the hydropathic practitioner in a striking manner. On a cold, foggy, unbearable day, such as we often experience in Europe, a patient, wet and weary, presents himself for cool or cold appliances. He is not warm enough for the particular process, and he has not spirit enough left to try to rouse up the circulation by open-air exercise. He is taken and prepared for the process by the Turkish bath, and sufficient heat developed in him to secure reaction after the process, which thus becomes altogether enjoyable, as well as effective. In this way the bath acts as a splendid counteractive to climate, and as a substitute for exercise.

By a judicious use of the Turkish bath hydropathy is put within the reach of almost everyone not suffering from an incurable organic disease, and even those would find alleviation from their sufferings. It enables all those suffering from rheumatism and diseases of the respiratory organs, as well as that large class known as "delicate people," and who are unable to take a sufficient amount of exercise in order to promote the perspiration necessary before cold or tepid water applications, to perspire easily and without exertion, thus securing for them the full benefit arising from cold or tepid water applications. The same might be said of thousands—nay, tens of thousands—whose occupations prevent them from taking regular daily exercise.

It is to be regretted that the Turkish bath has not yet found its way to Graefenberg, but I have every reason to believe that as Priessnitz's young and able grandson has now taken the management of the establishment into his own hands, and as there is every prospect that Graefenberg, which at present forms part of the Freiwaldau community, will shortly become an independent borough, it will not be long before the Turkish bath and a few other improvements, which, in the interest of the public, I have mentioned, will find their way to Graefenberg, thus reinstating it as the first and foremost hydropathic health resort in Austria and Central Europe.

I was sorry to notice that the practice established by Priessnitz of his patients having their

VILLA AUSTRIA.

CURHAUS ANNENHOF.

To face p. 144.

meals together in the common dining-hall has now fallen into disuse at Graefenberg.

Priessnitz considered it of the utmost importance that patients should have their meals under the immediate supervision of their doctor, and that no food should appear at the table but such as is suitable for invalids undergoing treatment.

Although this rule entailed upon Priessnitz, and especially upon his excellent wife, an immense amount of extra work, as well as of care and thought, he never would consent to any relaxation of it, but repeatedly rejected offers by which not only a great load of care and responsibility would have been removed, but considerable pecuniary advantage have been gained. The same rule prevails in our English hydropathic establishments, and the advantages arising from this practice are too obvious to require a detailed review.

At Graefenberg, at the present time, this important question is not sufficiently considered, and patients are allowed to choose their own restaurant. The lack of control over the cuisine of such restaurants, hotels and boarding and private houses as the numerous patients patronize must inevitably lead to many mistakes on the part of both visitor and caterer, which under Priessnitz's own plan would be more easily avoidable.

During Priessnitz's lifetime Graefenberg was difficult of access. There being no railway within a long distance of the place, invalids had to travel there by stage-coaches; but during the last fifteen or twenty years access to Graefenberg has been facilitated by a branch railway line. The accommodation at Graefenberg is still limited; the number of visitors is greatest during the summer months, and the major portion of them undergo the water-cure on similar lines to those followed in the time of Priessnitz. From what I could gather during my visit, the cases on the whole are not so severe now as in the time of Priessnitz.

For the benefit of English visitors to Graefenberg, we give a few hints as to the routes from London, as well as some local information.

There are two good routes from England, one viâ Breslau, the other viâ Vienna; the distance is about the same either way.

1. From Liverpool Street viâ Harwich, Hook of Holland, to Breslau, with option of stopping at Hamburg, Berlin or Dresden. From Breslau to Graefenberg is about five hours' journey by rail, stopping at the following places: Brieg, Neisse, Deutsch Wette, and Ziegenhals, the frontier town between Prussian and Austrian Silesia, and where the luggage is examined. From Ziegenhals to Freiwaldau (Graefenberg) is about an hour by rail.

RESTAURANT SCHINDLER.

DR. SCHINDLER'S CURHAUS.

To face p. 146.

2. Viâ Dover, Calais, Cologne, Vienna. From Vienna is about nine hours' journey by rail, stopping at Prerau, Olmütz, Sternberg and Haunsdorf to Freiwaldau.

Best Hotels at Freiwaldau.—Bahnhof Hotel (Station Hotel) ; Krone (Crown) keeps the best *table d'hôte* in the whole neighbourhood ; Kaiser von Oesterreich (Emperor of Austria) ; Kronprinz (Crown Prince), and others.

From Freiwaldau to Graefenberg is the distance of a twenty minutes' drive.

Principal Houses at Graefenberg.—The Annenhof (very good) ; the offices of the Kurcommission (bathing administration) are in this building. They give addresses of rooms and other information to visitors. Villa Adelheid (equally good ; same proprietor), with post and telegraph-office. (Five deliveries daily in summer, three in winter ; telegraphic service every day from 8 a.m. to 7 p.m.) Villa Austria ; Exners Curhaus ; Stefaniehof ; Villa Silesia, Villa Polonia, and many others. Belonging to the Priessnitz family are Grosses Curhaus (large curehouse), with inspector's office. If visitors prefer living in one of the five Priessnitz houses, they must apply at this office. This large building has thirty-eight good rooms ; reading-rooms, where the administration keeps for the use of visitors more than forty daily papers and magazines in different languages ; a circulating library of about five thousand volumes; and an assembly hall (Kursaal). This beautiful hall is the identical large dining-hall used by Priessnitz, and which is mentioned in his " Life." Neues Curhaus, having the best hydropathic appliances in Graefenberg; Priessnitz Geburtshaus (native place), surrounded by a pretty garden.

There are also several houses belonging to Dr. Schindler's widow. They are five in number, with fine and extensive grounds, besides several other houses.

An excellent private road, the Hughanweg, ascends up to the forest. Half-way up stands the fine Hughan Castle, the property of Mrs. Louisa Hughan, a wealthy and charitable lady, for many years a summer resident at Graefenberg.

Amusements.—A special committee, chosen by the visitors, takes charge of the arrangements for concerts, theatricals, dances, picnics, etc. The large Kursaal in the Grosses Curhaus is used for this purpose, and has a piano kept for the use of visitors.

Sometimes the building erected by the late Grand Duke of Mecklenburg is used. It boasts of a beautiful Kegelbahn (bowling-place), a gift from the same august personage.

A band plays twice a day in the stand on the promenade, and in wet weather at the Kursaal.

Cur-taxes.—It is a general custom in Continental

HUGHAN CASTLE.

To face p. 148.

watering-places to levy (by order of the local administration) a small tax on every visitor, to defray general expenses, such as the band, keeping in good order and embellishing the place, etc. A percentage of 15 per cent. to 20 per cent. is devoted to the support of the local poor.

For visitors exceeding a stay of five days at Graefenberg proper : 15s. for one person, 22s. for two persons, and 28s. for three or more persons belonging to the same family. At the Colony, Freiwaldau, and Boehmischdorf, 7s., 11s., and 13s. respectively.

There is no central place for treatment at Graefenberg, as is the case in most other hydros. Every house has its special water-service, direct from the springs, and on each floor are bath-rooms as well as movable baths, which are easily wheeled in and out of bedrooms. Sitz-baths at Graefenberg are always given in bedrooms.

Three doctors (hydropathists) practise at Graefenberg : Dr. Eduard Emmel, at the Annenhof, all the year round; Dr. Hosann, at the Grosses Curhaus, all the year ; Dr. Rudolph Habschek, at the Doctorhaus, from May to October.

CHAPTER XI

RECENT HYDROPATHY

IN these times of feverish activity, when events follow each other with almost startling rapidity, we are apt to forget those to whose life-work and unselfish devotion the world owes its advancement. Our debt of gratitude to their memory we can only in part repay by handing down to posterity the knowledge of our benefactor's life-work in all its integrity.

Priessnitz was a man of genius, one of the few distinguished men of this century.

Let us recall to mind the almost complete ignorance of the world sixty years ago regarding the ordinary elementary laws of hygiene.

Cleanliness in its wider sense, diet, out-of-door exercise, well-ventilated dwellings, etc., were, to the majority of people, the wealthier classes not excepted, nothing but meaningless words.

It would be out of place to draw a true picture of the state of abject misery of the inhabitants of the poorer quarters of our large towns, and how diseases in their most terrible form decimated our over - crowded cities. And unfortunately things were not much better in many rural districts.

What did the majority of the medical faculty do to improve such a state of things ? Did the reckless use of medicines help to strengthen enfeebled constitutions, or did those innumerable salves, ointments, and decoctions restore life and activity to the emaciated limbs due to long physical suffering ? And, worst of all, what was the result on the sufferer's shattered frame of that too common practice of blood-letting, and of the abuse of alcoholic stimulants ?

Far from alleviating sufferings, the common use of powerful medicines increased them tenfold. What wonder that people, in their helplessness and despair, resorted to that curse of mankind, excessive alcoholic drink ?

A small tenant farmer's son was destined to promote the great work of regeneration, and we have seen how nobly he responded to this Divine mission ; how, far from the noise and turmoil of the great world, he devoted his life to the study and practice of treating diseased persons by hygienic means.

Envy and wounded vanity have been unable to suppress the facts that Priessnitz was the first to systematize and promote a new method of healing, and that his system of treatment has achieved the most wonderful success. In looking back to former attempts at employing the water-cure, for instance, to the often successful cures achieved by the two Hahns, father and son, during the first half of last century, scientific men will only be more confirmed in their admiration of Priessnitz's marvellous power.

He overcame the many difficulties with which his path was strewn, restoring thousands and tens of thousands to health, activity, and vigour, and leaving behind him a system of hygienic medicine which was perfect as far as it went, because it acquiesced with the laws of organic welfare.

The benefits arising from his ministrations are felt by all classes of society. To him we owe the *erection of the first public bath and wash-houses in England.**

If posterity should ever wish to honour by a special mark of distinction those good and noble men who have been a blessing to humanity, it

---

* One of Priessnitz's patients, a man of prominent position in the city of London, who had been cured at Graefenberg, was one of the first to agitate for the "Baths and Wash-houses" movement in this country. This gentleman attended a meeting at the Mansion House held by the Lord Mayor in 1844, which resulted in the establishment of the first public baths and wash-houses in Glasshouse Yard, London.

certainly will not forget the great Silesian physician.

The life of this man became, so to say, the symbol of what ought to be the life of a re-generated race. Men of our time must learn to recognise and respect the simple laws of natural life which make toward organic welfare.

The life-work of Vincent Priessnitz presents some cogent facts, viz. :

Firstly, that many complaints can be treated effectually by measures not recognised in our schools of medicine, and by men with no medical degrees.

Secondly, that a good deal of so-called quackery is a direct result of medical colleges not ad-mitting and fairly trying any innovation that has been developed either by accident or from scientific investigation.

Thirdly, if medical professors were to turn their attention more to hydrotherapeutics, and less to physic, there would be less opportunity for so-called quackery to trespass upon their preserves.

There is a disposition in the various medical colleges throughout Europe to raise the standard of medical examination. But, judging from the past, this move is no evidence that the public at large are going to derive any more benefit than they have done since the days of Hippocrates, *i.e.*, so far as hygienic remedies are concerned.

153

In fact, I am afraid it will only make the coming students more intolerant than their predecessors regarding the simpler remedial measures. On the Continent, and in America, the medical faculty are more favourably disposed towards hydropathy than in the British Isles.

I am pleased to see that Professor Kussmaul, at the last sessions held at Heidelberg in 1896, refused to sign the programme drawn up for medical examinations owing to the paper not containing hydrotherapeutic questions. Professor Kussmaul has given his reasons in a pamphlet,* a review of which appeared in the *Echo*, London, December, 1896, which I append :

" The Nestor of German medicine, the famous Professor and Privy Councillor Adolf Kussmaul, of Heidelberg, has not a little startled his colleagues by withholding his signature from the new programme drawn up by the commissioners for medical examinations.

" In a short pamphlet explaining his reasons for his dissent, the professor throws the whole weight of his authority into the scale of hydropathy. It is not so much for what the new programme contains, as for what it omits, says Dr. Kussmaul, that he is unwilling to set his seal to it. The time has come, he contends, in which every young

* Adolf Kussmaul, Emer. Professor der Universitat Strassburg. "Ueber den kommissarischen Entwurf zur Revision der deutscher medizinischen Prüfungsordnung Heidelberg." Carl Winter's Universitätsbuchhandlung, 1897, 8vo., pp. 24 and wrapper.

physician ought to be thoroughly schooled in the priceless therapeutic value and application of water, and in the scarcely less momentous function of pure air, in the healing of disease. ' It is not only among the educated,' writes the learned pathologist, ' but amongst all ranks of the people, that a justifiable suspicion of drugs has now penetrated. The physician's recipe is now declining in credit and favour, and the old shyness of water and fresh air disappearing, and the conviction everywhere increasing that the most effective means of hygiene lie in three simple things rightly understood and applied—air, water, and diet.'

" The aged professor, who has lectured in his time to so many thousands of medical apprentices, gives a lively sketch of the young doctor, when his education is supposed to be finished, going forth from the university and the schools to his work. ' He can diagnose exactly and correctly; he can distinguish precisely a dozen sorts of *bakterien* from one another; he is completely skilled in his knowledge of the contents of the chemical kitchen; he can administer with dexterity the minimal and maximal doses of the most dangerous alkaloids; the *morpheum spiritze* accompanies him in all his goings out and comings in. But of hydropathy our young doctor, when he leaves the schools, knows nothing at all.'

" Professor Kussmaul then pictures the conscientious young doctor as struck with amazement and vexation at the discovery that some patient, whom his skill and science have failed to help, has been cured by a water-doctor, who has enjoyed no medical training, and whom he can only regard as a pretender and quack.

" ' Here,' continues Dr. Kussmaul, ' lies the

weak point of our medical training. A revision of the method and order of our studies is a pressing necessity. Water has gained the favour and confidence of the public in spite of us. Water, in combination with a skilful dietetic treatment, is the one great demand of the nerves, of the blood, of the breathing, of the physiological system in countless acute and chronic ailments.'

" It is certainly symptomatic of something like a medical revolution, that a man of such great distinction as a teacher and writer on pathology in his old age, and as the result of arduous scientific researches, should liberate himself so boldly from the conservative traditions of his profession. One thing may be regarded with satisfaction—the drug-doctor, propped up as he is by organization within, and general newspaper authority from without, is doomed."

The time for questioning the remedial efficacy of hydropathy is past. Evidences of its therapeutic power are to be met with everywhere in the form of healthy Englishmen and Englishwomen, whose ailments, apparently intractable, disappeared under its kindly influence.

It is, however, generally supposed that its efficacy is confined to those districts where mountain air lends its aid in the treatment of disease. Many persons who can vouch for having received signal benefit from hydropathy have to add that they sought its aid, if not amid the hills of Austrian Silesia, where Priessnitz made his wonderful cures, at any rate in some hilly country, it may be of

Scotland, or Ireland, or of Worcestershire, Derby-shire, or Yorkshire. And not unnaturally, perhaps, it is supposed that only in such places is the water-cure likely to be of benefit.

Were this supposition correct, the field of usefulness open to hydropathy would be of com-paratively small extent. Only the rich could take advantage of it. Of the pent-up inhabitants of our large towns, who, of all people, most need hydropathic appliances, not more than two or three per cent. could go where they were to be had.

But is this supposition correct? We answer most assuredly " No." While we admit that pure mountain air is one of the best of restoratives, we must deny that hydropathy needs it more than any other mode of treatment. And, further, we maintain that no other therapeutic system can do so well without this help, inasmuch as its measures do more than any other to oxygenate the blood, and to supply the place of mountain air.

To clear up this point a little, let us revert to the origin of the water-cure. It "hails," as the Americans would say, from Graefenberg, a very healthy, mountainous district, which we have already described. This, however, was but a chance circumstance. It might just as well have "hailed" from Putney, Poplar, or " Little Ped-lington." The facts of the case are these: Priessnitz was born and brought up in the Graefenberg district, and, like all his neighbours, was, in case of accident or disease, treated in the ordinary way.

It so happened, however, that Priessnitz, while suffering from the effects of a severe accident, was declared by his medical attendant to be beyond the hope of recovery. Having had a little previous experience in the use of wet bandages and douchings, our patient resolved to try what hydropathic treatment could do in this serious crisis. He made a trial, and his trial was crowned with success. Wet bandages skilfully applied cured him.

Then he began to treat his neighbours in their accidents or diseases, and here, too, he was successful. It became evident that hydropathic appliances were better than ordinary medical means, and so they came to be preferred.

This, however, had nothing to do with the character of the district as respects soil, scenery, air, population, or anything else. The district was the same for both systems of treatment ; and if the water-treatment proved the better, it must have been owing to some virtue in itself. If the virtue, then, be in the treatment itself, one locality will do for it just as well as another—the heart of a great city just as well as the brow of a great mountain.

That Priessnitz was of this opinion appears from

the fact that after his fame had spread throughout Europe, and people came to Graefenberg from all quarters, he did not confine his practice of hydropathy to that healthy region, but visited and treated patients at their own homes in towns, where similar success attended his manipulations.

There are some who would stultify Priessnitz by making his saying, " Man muss Gebirge haben " (One must have mountains), to mean that he considered a mountainous region indispensable to the successful practice of hydropathy. But, as the facts above stated show, the whole career of Priessnitz gives the lie to such a notion. His meaning was simply this: that mountain air was a very fine air for the health of men and animals. In the same sense it may, with equal truth, be said that " we must have plains and valleys," since if a country without hills is unhealthy, a country without plains and valleys is barren, and it will be of small benefit to either men or animals if the mountain air gives them appetite while the soil yields but a scanty fare.

There can be no doubt that it was in some respects a misfortune to the cause of hydropathy that such a locality as Graefenberg was the birthplace of the system, for the cases occurring in the neighbourhood were of course few, and only the wealthy could afford to come from a distance. Had the system been developed in a town or populous district, the wider diffusion of the benefits attending it, the enlarged experience gained, the new facts and principles brought to light, and the energetic lay and professional support enlisted, would all have told in favour of its adoption and advancement. As a result, we should in all likelihood have first become acquainted with hydropathy through the medium of our hospitals, in which its measures would have proved a great boon: if they had not quite superseded ordinary medication, they would have found their way into general practice.

As things have turned out, there has been a putting of the cart before the horse, inasmuch as hydropathy has been pressed upon the public by laymen, while the public have, in their turn, compelled the profession in some measure to recognise its claims.

There is no reason why water-treatment should not be practised in our large centres of the population just as well as drug-treatment, each application producing certain medical results immaterially, whether it is on the hills of Scotland or in St. Giles's.

The same causes that bring on disease in the country bring it on in the town, viz., unhealthy habits and unhealthy surroundings, and the water-cure, which at once assails these causes, and which at Graefenberg proved its great superiority to other treatment, is surely competent to deal with their effects, wherever they may show themselves.

To Priessnitz, who never caused a line to be written on his behalf, we are indebted for the methodical development of the water-cure. He energetically and quietly pursued a course of action of his own in dealing with human ailments, and the wide fame he acquired during his life was owing to the cures of chronic diseases where other remedial measures had failed. It may be truly said that the unpopularity of hydrotherapeutics with the medical faculty in England is mainly due to the fear of breaking up their old machinery; but the time will come, sooner or later, when they will have to recognise Priessnitz's remedies in their schools of medicine. In Germany and Austria the system has in a measure triumphed over the complicated pharmaceutical medicaments, and is being largely employed by general practitioners. Unfortunately a large proportion of our medical men of the old school look upon hydropathy as quackery. I am quite prepared to admit that there is as much quackery outside the medical profession as within, but it must be borne in mind that the distinction between quacks and respectable practitioners is one not so much of the remedies used as of knowledge, of skill, and of honesty in using them.

Dr. Lauder Brunton, referring in a course of

lectures* to the wet-sheet pack, says, on page 122 : " The most striking example that I ever saw of the use of cold water was in the case of a patient suffering from pneumonia who was dying from hyperpyrexia, without anyone knowing it, for it was before the days of clinical thermometers in this country.

" The patient was under the care of the late Professor J. Hughes Bennett, whose boast it was that he had never lost a case of uncomplicated pneumonia since the time that he had discarded the old method of blood-letting, and began that of simply supporting the patient's strength. One day, on going round, he was a good deal disgusted to find that one of his patients suffering from double pneumonia was apparently about to spoil his statistics by dying. The man was completely comatose, and apparently moribund. It seemed as if nothing possibly could be done to help him, and Professor Bennett was passing on to the next bed when a Swedish doctor named Scolberg, who happened to be attending Bennett's clinic, said to the professor : ' May I treat the patient, Professor Bennett ?' ' You can do what you like with him,' was the answer. Forthwith Scolberg

* Lauder Brunton (T.), "Lectures on the Action of Medicines : being the Course of Lectures on Pharmacology and Therapeutics delivered at St. Bartholomew's Hospital during the Summer Session of 1896." London : Macmillan and Co., 1897.

ordered in a big tub of cold water. All the bed-
clothes were pulled off. A wet-sheet was dipped
in the water, and the patient was wrapped in it.
In a few minutes it was taken off, and a second
cold sheet applied. How long this went on I
do not know, because, like all the rest who were
watching the process, I thought that it was
useless, and I went away to have my lunch. On
going back about an hour afterwards, simply from
curiosity to see whether the man were dead or
not, I was greatly astonished, instead of finding
an empty bed as I expected, to see the patient
lying quiet and comfortable, apparently in an easy
slumber, and he went on from that time forward
without a bad symptom, and recovered perfectly
in due course. So a wet-sheet simply wrung out
of cold water, put upon the patient for a short
time, taken off again, dipped again, and frequently
renewed, tends to bring down the patient's
temperature."

Sir William Broadbent, writing on fever,*
states : "Of special measures for the reduction
of febrile heat when this is becoming dangerous,
either from its intensity or duration, the first to
be mentioned is the cool or cold bath. This
should be resorted to in all cases of hyperpyrexia,

* Quain (Sir R.), "A Dictionary of Medicine," by various
writers. Seventeenth thousand. London: Longmans, 1892.
Part I., article "Fever," pp. 511, 512.

from whatever cause ; its efficacy, first established in the high temperature of acute rheumatism and enteric fever, has been proved also in cases of septic hyperpyrexia after ovariotomy, and even in injuries to the brain. Here the water may be positively cold. When the bath is employed to control temperature, not dangerous from its height, but from its duration, as in enteric fever, it need not be lower than 70° or 65° Fahr."

The late Sir John Forbes wrote of hydropathy as follows :

" The water-cure is a stomachic, since it invariably increases the appetite.

" It is a *local calefacient* in the wet - sheet, covered by dry blankets and mackintosh.

" It is derivative; cold friction at one part, by exciting increased action there, produces corresponding diminution elsewhere, the compress frequently acting, if not like a blister, at least like a mustard poultice.

" It is a local as well as a general counter-irritant.

" It is essentially alterative in the continued renewal of old matter ; its renewal is shown in the maintenance of the same weight."

The late Dr. John Goodman very graphically compares the hydropathic treatment with the allopathic remedies and their supposed medical actions. I reprint this comparison with some alterations :

"*Allopathic Alteratives.*—Mercury, iodine, pot·assæ hydriod., antimony, sarsaparilla.

"*Hydropathic Alteratives.*—Wet-sheet packings, local and general, hot-air baths, cold and cool effusions.

"*Allopathic Antiphlogistics.*—Alkalies and neutral salts, calomel, antimony, venesection, leeches.

"*Hydropathic Antiphlogistics* are wet-sheet packings of short duration, tepid baths, ablutions, hot fomentations, fever compresses, and long-continued sitz-baths.

"*Allopathic Anodynes.*—White poppy, lactuca, humulus.

"*Hydropathic Anodynes.*—For nerve pain, wet friction and ablution, streams of water, douchings, dripping-sheets, and half-baths, wet packing and ablution, hot mustard spinal washes, followed by gradual pail douches, wet compress to liver and spine, with sweating-baths. Diet chiefly vegetable, but nutritious.

"*Allopathic Diaphoretics.*—Antimonials, ipecacuanha, neutral salts, liq. ammon. acet., Dover's powder.

"*Hydropathic Diaphoretics.*—Cold-water drinks, hot ditto, wet-sheet packings, dripping-sheets, cooling compresses, hot-air bath, with or without moisture.

"*Allopathic Counter-Irritants and Derivatives.*—In medicine external appliances, issues and setons, blisters, moxas, stimulant embrocations, cataplasms, and other irritants, mustard cataplasms to the feet in fevers, application of leeches to distant parts, etc. There is no remedy in medicine that can act as a *general derivative* except the warm bath with mustard.

" *Hydropathic Counter-Irritants and Derivatives* are mustard sheet-packs, chillis, and Coote's acetic acid rubbed into the body, mustard rubbed into the parts affected, hot brine, local and general warm baths, hot air or sulphur, vapour baths with cold or cool effusions.

" *Allopathic Diuretics.*—Squills, digitalis, nitric ether, acetate of potash, broom-tops, dandelion, mercury.

" *Hydropathic Diuretics.*—Copious water-drinking, hot-air baths, sitz-baths, wet packing, etc. No remedies act more powerfully on the kidneys without injury. Copious drinking of barley-water is good.

" *Allopathic Expectorants.*—Ipecacuanha, mercury, antimonials, squills, balsam of tolu.

" *Hydropathic Expectorants.*—Mild ablution of cold or tepid water chest-washings, graduated according to debility of the case, chest compresses worn constantly. Wet-sheet packing, mustard trunk-packing, mild Turkish baths, liquid sulphur shallow bath, wet hand-rubbing, and tepid sitz-baths.

"*Allopathic Aperients—Cathartics.*—Manna, magnesia, rhubarb, confection of senna, sulphur, sulphate of magnesia, calomel, colocynth.

"*Hydropathic Aperients.*—Water-drinking, water enemas, wet-covered abdominal or spino-abdominal compresses, and abdominal washings. Sitz-bath, pail douche on the spine and abdomen, wet-sheet packings and douching of the abdomen, shallow baths, etc. Exercise regularly taken. Diet : Brown bread and oatmeal, ripe fruits, etc.

"*Allopathic Narcotics.* — Opium, belladonna, conium, hyoscyamus.

"*Hydropathic Narcotics.*—No remedy sooner procures sleep than the wet-sheet packing and hot fomentations to the stomach and bowels. The tepid sitz-bath or general ablution at bedtime is an admirable sleep-producer.

"*Allopathic Tonics.*—Bark, iron, quinine, gentian, columba, mineral acids.

"*Hydropathic Tonics.*—Pure cold water is the greatest tonic to the stomach that can be taken. It dissolves obstacles in the intestine, and gives tone. Water being easily absorbed, it easily enters into the blood, and rapidly dissolves foreign matter, which is readily carried off by the excretory organs. No remedies are equal to cool or cold baths as tonics in chronic diseases and general debility. If judiciously prescribed and employed they never disagree, but act on the whole body, producing increased vital energy in every organ, and entire renewal of the whole man to the extent of which the constitutional powers are capable."

Such is a comparative view of the leading hydropathic and allopathic methods, after a study of which the reader will be able to form an opinion of their respective merits as medical agents designed to alleviate human sufferings.

The late Dr. Carpenter, Professor of Physiology in the Royal Institution, says that the wet-sheet pack used by the hydropathist is one of the most powerful of all diaphoretics, and no person who has watched its operations can deny that it is a very valuable remedy. If its agency be fairly tested, there is strong reason to believe that it will be found to be the most valuable curative means we possess in specific nervous diseases, which depend upon the presence of morbid matter in the blood, especially gout and chronic rheumatism, as well as that depressed state of the general system which results from the wear and tear of the body and mental powers.

Dr. Wilson counts the wet-sheet pack as an antiphlogistic, or means of subduing fever in its hot stage with active circulation. In this respect it stands unrivalled, being unequalled in its simplicity, safety, and efficacy. It is certainly the noblest arm of the water-cure, causing little or no loss of strength, and leaving behind it none of the debility which bleeding and strong medicines occasion. Dr. Wilson puts the action of the pack in a nutshell when he says: " It effectually abstracts the morbid heat of the system, and reduces the excited, nervous, and vascular actions, producing all the coolness and calm necessary for the moment, and by the very nature of this process the degree of extraction of heat is fixed."

The first Lord Lytton, in his " Confessions of a Water - Patient " (*New Monthly Magazine*, London, 1845), writes of the wet-sheet pack as follows: " The first momentary chill is promptly succeeded by a gradual and vivifying warmth, perfectly free from the irritation of dry heat; a delicious sense of ease is usually followed by a sleep more agreeable than anodynes ever produced. *It seems a positive cruelty to be relieved from this magic girdle in which pain is lulled and fever cooled, and wakefulness lapped in slumber.*"

CHAPTER XII

RECENT HYDROPATHY—*continued*

PRIESSNITZ no sooner began to astonish the world by his successes than he had imitators and disciples. We read that in 1839 as many as one hundred and twenty doctors went to Graefenberg to study the water-cure.

Amongst the more successful of Priessnitz's pupils were Munde, Rausse, and Schindler.

Rausse was the most energetic in propagating the new method of healing in Germany. Munde founded the first hydropathic establishment in America, while Schindler became the master's worthy successor at Graefenberg.

Dr. Josef Schindler was born on July 29, 1814. After having studied for some time at Graefenberg, he became convinced of the importance of the water-cure as a remedial agent, and he resolved to renounce the practice of allopathy. Although attacked from all sides, nothing shook his convictions, nor was the opposition of his relations and

DR. JOSEPH SCHINDLER.

To face p. 170.

friends able to alter his opinion. In 1839 he founded a hydropathic establishment at Tiefenbach, in the Iser Mountains of Bohemia, where he made many useful experiments. At the age of forty, after Priessnitz's death, he was asked to take the direction of the Graefenberg establishment, and at the end of March, 1852, he went to Graefenberg to continue his great friend and master's work.

He united a rare modesty to an even rarer unselfishness, resembling Priessnitz himself in this respect, as well as in some peculiarities of manner. He could, however, only proceed gradually with improving or modifying any of the established methods, as certain people were so enthusiastic in their admiration of Priessnitz as to reject all innovation as wrong and harmful.

In 1858 Schindler, with the help of Baron L. von der Decken-Himmelreich, published a periodical for the propagation of the method of healing and the care of health in general, based on all natural means, called "Communications from Graefenberg," which became popular, and won many physicians to the method. His lectures on health were interesting and successful, because Schindler understood how to impart his knowledge in a simple and unostentatious manner.

The number of his pupils was great, and some of them have risen to distinction.

Schindler's great merit consisted in having not only kept intact Priessnitz's original method of proceeding, but also in having improved it in various ways. He died, deeply regretted, on March 8, 1890.

It may be added that the Grand Duke of Mecklenburg-Schwerin gave to his "dear Dr. Schindler" the gold medal *litteris et artibus*.

Amongst other pioneers in the movement was Dr. Joseph Weiss. Weiss was born in 1795 at Breitenfurt, studied medicine in Vienna, and practised later in different parts of Austria, finally settling at Freiwaldau.

He soon perceived the far-reaching importance of Priessnitz's system, and after studying it with care, he founded a hydro at Freiwaldau. This was in 1835. His establishment enjoyed great popularity until 1841, when Weiss was invited to England to found one of the first hydropathic establishments in this country, at Stand Steadbury, in Hertfordshire, where he administered personally till the autumn of 1843.

In the following year he founded a new hydro at Sudbrook Park, Richmond, Surrey. His health, however, broke down, and in 1845 he confided the direction of the establishment to a friend, hoping to regain his health by a visit to the Continent, and then to resume his duties at Sudbrook Park. He died, however, of acute gout, at Freiwaldau, in 1847.

KALTENLEUTGEBEN, NEAR VIENNA.

To face p. 172.

His " Handbook on Hydropathy" appeared in English, and was one of the first treatises on hydropathy on a scientific basis. The University of Oxford conferred upon the author, as an acknowledgment of the merits of this work, the title of Honorary Doctor. He was the author of several other works on hydropathy in German.

Another early pupil of the founder of hydropathy was Dr. Raisnick, who studied at Graefenberg, came to England, and became the consulting physician at Ben Rhydding (opened in 1844).

Another Priessnitz student was Dr. Johann Emmel, whose work led to important results. He made, in 1835, the experiment of forming a "Priessnitz Establishment " at Kaltenleutgeben, a beautiful valley in the Wienerwald, a finely-wooded tract within a short distance of Vienna. At first, however, the difficulties were so great, partly owing to the prejudice of the authorities, that the place was closed. But it was soon re-opened in consequence of the kindly intervention of the Empress Maria Anna, and since that time the Emmel establishment has made steady progress from year to year. It has, however, never attained to the magnitude and importance of the hydropathic establishment founded in this romantic valley by Professor Winternitz in June, 1865.

Dr. Winternitz was born on March 1, 1835, at Josefstadt, in Bohemia. In 1858 he accompanied the Empress of Austria to Corfu; somewhat later he practised in Prague as specialist in mental diseases, and after that became assistant to Oppolzer and Dulek. After having studied hydropathy at Graefenberg, he founded his establishment at Kaltenleutgeben. At that time Kaltenleutgeben was but a modest little place, ignorant, so to speak, of its own resources. It then contained only one hundred and twenty cottages, and there are now two hundred and forty-five more or less substantial houses, many of them very good indeed, in addition to which the place has most of the conveniences of modern civilization, well-lit streets, good restaurants, a public library, etc.

Kaltenleutgeben has for many years been a favourite resort of the Viennese people. Latterly, with increasing comforts and conveniences, the number of visitors has become more and more considerable, especially since the construction of a branch line has placed it in connection with the Austrian Southern Railway. Its chief importance, however, lies in the fact of its being the most considerable hydropathic establishment in Austria, next to Graefenberg.

In 1865 the Winternitz establishment contained only fifteen patients. Since then the number has gone on steadily increasing, until at the present moment there are twenty-one houses, with accommodation for three hundred and twenty patients.

To face p. 174.

PROFESSOR WINTERNITZ' CURHAUS, KALTENLEUTGEBEN, NEAR VIENNA.

To face p. 174 b.

RECENT HYDROPATHY

Kaltenleutgeben occupies the foremost rank amongst hydropathic establishments. This must be ascribed in the first place to the scientific eminence of its founder, and in the second place to its unexceptionable hygienic position. Able managers are constantly adding to the comfort and convenience of the community there. The air is so pure and healthy that cholera has never penetrated this valley. A cross erected at the foot of the Gaisberg bears witness to this fact. Dr. Winternitz's experience and knowledge have raised the establishment to its present state of prosperity, and his authority as a hydropathist is now so widely recognised as to ensure absolute success to any undertaking in which he may engage. During the space of a quarter of a century 12,800 patients have visited Kaltenleutgeben. Seven hundred and thirty-five patients visited the establishment in 1896.

It consists of fourteen villas and houses, three large kur- and bath-houses, an institute for health gymnastics, massage, and electric treatment, besides several other buildings, amongst which are the beautifully-fitted and admirably-managed Kursaal, with reading and writing-rooms, a recreation-room, and a music-room.

The water-appliances as used at the hydro at Kaltenleutgeben are essentially the same as adopted by Priessnitz, with additions on a more scientific basis. Professor Dr. Winternitz is, moreover, the inventor of a number of entirely new hydropathic appliances well known and used throughout Germany.

Besides the application of electric baths, Swedish gymnastics, massage, etc., diet is, in Dr. Winternitz's establishment, considered of great importance, such as the milk-cure, vegetable-cure, Weir-Mitchell cure, etc.

Ziemssen's words convey the true expression of the recognition of the merits of Professor Winternitz from a scientific and professional point of view: "We owe to Winternitz the greater part of what we call to-day scientific hydrotherapy." He is an Imperial Councillor and a Member of the Administration of the Poloklinik at Vienna. He is the possessor of numerous decorations, and is an honorary member of several medical societies. His book, "Hydrotherapy," is the most important work of its kind.

Having made mention of Dr. Johann Emmel, the founder of the first hydropathic establishment at Kaltenleutgeben, it would be an unpardonable omission to overlook his talented son, Dr. Emanuel Emmel, who has followed in his father's footsteps, and is an enthusiastic disciple of the water-treatment. He never took medicine of any kind; in two serious illnesses, which brought him almost to death's door, he was cured by the

DR. EDOUARD EMMEL.

To face p. 176.

water-treatment, and is convinced of the excellence of the method.

Emmel had been designed from his early youth to become his father's successor in the medical profession. Circumstances, however, forced him, after having completed his academical studies, to enter the Austrian army. He took part in the war of 1866. On his return, after the close of the war, he fell ill again, and was obliged to retire from active service. Once more the water-cure was the means of restoring him to perfect health.

Nothing now prevented Emmel from giving himself up entirely to the study of medicine, and he qualified at Vienna.

The study of medicine did not diminish Emmel's belief in the water-treatment, although he was of opinion that in order to practise hydropathy with success a thorough knowledge of anatomy, physiology, and pathology is indispensable.

Dr. Emmel is now one of the resident doctors at Graefenberg, a position which he has held for some years, following in the footsteps of his two great predecessors, Priessnitz and Schindler.

He is the author of a widely-known practical manual on hydropathy.

An account of the progress of hydropathy on the Continent would be incomplete without some reference to Dr. Beni-Barde, who may be justly designated the leader of scientific hydrotherapy in

France. Indeed, he occupies the same position in that country that Professor Winternitz does in Austria. He has improved and enlarged his talented predecessor Dr. Fleury's somewhat imperfect method, and through patient research has raised hydrotherapy to its present prominent position in France.

In 1860 Dr. Beni-Barde took the direction of Dr. Fleury's hydropathic establishment at Bellevue, where he remained till 1865.

In that year he became director of the hydropathic establishment at Auteuil, Paris, which position he held until 1880.

In 1876 Dr. Beni - Barde founded a model establishment of his own in Paris — Rue de Miromesnil—the water being supplied by an Artesian well thirty-five metres deep.

The establishment contains every hydrotherapeutic appliance useful in nervous and chronic diseases.

Dr. Beni-Barde has annexed to his establishment, under the direction of Professor D'Arsonval, an electro-therapeutic installation, including special electric baths, the solenoid, electric massage, etc. Dr. Beni-Barde is consulting physician of the hydropathic establishment at Auteuil, near the Bois de Boulogne, where the patients are sent who require the combined advantages of pure fresh air, quiet, and rest, together with therapeutic treatment.

DR. BENI-BARDE.

To face p. 178.

DR. BENI-BARDE'S ESTABLISHMENT AT AUTEUIL, NEAR PARIS.

To face p. 178 n.

Dr. J. M. A. Beni-Barde is the author of several works on hydrotherapy, amongst which the foremost is: " Theoretical and Practical Treatise on Hydrotherapy, applied in Nervous and Chronic Diseases." (In French ; Paris, 1874.)

The Auteuil establishment comprises three detached buildings, which enable patients to choose rooms of whatever aspect they may prefer. An extensive garden, with beautiful old trees, ensures the enjoyment of fresh air and quiet. No mental cases are admitted.

There is an association, or union of associations, which has branches and little knots of members all through Germany and Austria. It is named the Health Society, and is a direct outcome of the teachings of Priessnitz. Its membership is composed of those who are " in favour of a mode of life and treatment in illness based only on the laws of Nature," and they are counted by thousands.

These societies, which in 1872 included only nine affiliated branches, in 1895 numbered 393 branch societies with 49,170 members.

Each member pays a small sum yearly to the funds of the association, for which he gets a very substantial return in the form of a gratis " cure " at one of the association's establishments in case of sickness. The association issues an illustrated monthly periodical entitled the *Naturarzt* (the Nature Doctor), which has nearly sixty thousand readers. In other ways the association does much for the propagation of ideas in regard to hydropathy and kindred subjects, including the delivery of free lectures to small societies.

Every two years the association holds a general meeting or congress, at which all the societies are represented by delegates. Papers are read, new ideas are discussed, and, of course, as the general public are invited to be present, much valuable information on important matters appertaining to life and health is disseminated. Would that in these matters we were as far advanced in this country, and that it were possible to hold biennial conferences on the subject of popular hygiene !

I add some particulars of what has become known as " Schroth's dietetic and hydrotherapic treatment."

The system is hydropathic, inasmuch as beyond dieting the wet-sheet pack is the only remedial agent used.

Johann Schroth was born at Boehmischdorf on February 11, 1798. He was a contemporary of Priessnitz, and distantly related to him. He lived the life of a farmer, and died in 1856.

In 1817 he fractured his knee-joint on falling from his horse. His treatment for this injury

JOHANN SCHROTH.

To face p. 180.

led to the evolution of his system of treating disease.

The Schroth system is carried out in his establishment at Lindewiese in Silesia. His son, Emanuel Schroth, conducted the establishment after his father's death until 1890. From five to six hundred patients are treated at the establishment every year. The system is simple, and can easily be followed at home. Patients, when beginning the semi-starvation diet, think that they will die under it, but they do not: they improve in health and strength.

The originality of the treatment consists in the way in which the wet-sheet pack is used. It is administered in conjunction with a spare vegetable diet and systematic white-wine drinking. The whole organism is dealt with on a defined system. Individual conditions of body and separate diseases are all treated similarly. The various local and general symptoms of disease are but little considered, unless they menace the patient's life.

The diseases more especially amenable to the treatment are those arising :

1. From inertness of the skin as an excretory organ ;

2. From imperfect assimilation of food ;

3. From specific poisons that have entered the body from without.

Schroth argues that in all these cases the body

has become a store - house for poisonous and morbid matter.

The main principle of the treatment is acceleration of tissue waste and of tissue renewal.

Moist heat is used to promote and regulate the functional activity of the excretory organs. The strict treatment is stimulating, and aims at inducing a "feverish" condition of body, with the object of wasting away tissue.

The chief difficulty in administering the treatment consists in adjusting for each patient the quantity and strength of the wine taken, and the rate of drinking, so as to allow due time for its absorption in such a manner as to maintain such a degree of "feverishness" in the patient for such length of time as may be necessary for the elimination of all morbid matters and structure from the body whilst maintaining due and healthier tissue renewal.

The Preparatory Treatment consists during the first week :

1. In patients sleeping all night in a wet-sheet pack. The arms are usually left free, and the sheet is fourfold in thickness around the trunk. In the morning the whole body is thoroughly rubbed with a warm, dry towel, and the patient remains in bed for half an hour afterwards. For the morning ablution only tepid water is used.

2. In using a spare vegetable diet, consisting

LINDEWIESE.

To face p. 182.

of one meal a day, the mid-day dinner, this being of one dish only, a dryish soup, thick enough to be eaten with a fork. It is made of grain or pulse with butter or salt. Wheaten rolls lightly baked are eaten in the morning, and when desired at other times.

3. In drinking non-alcoholic tepid drinks, such as barley-gruel, slightly sweetened and flavoured with lemon, and only taken to quench decided thirst.

During the second week, in addition to the above, a glass of hot white wine, mixed with half a glass of water and sweetened, is sipped between 3 and 4 p.m., whilst wheaten rolls are being eaten. The wine is drunk hot, but not boiled ; must be good and pure, but not old. The wine must be sipped slowly, one glass per half-hour.

During the third week the afternoon wine must be taken without the water, and two glasses are to be taken instead of one.

This preparatory treatment is lengthened or shortened, according to the nature of the illness and the character of the patient.

Strict Treatment.—This differs from the preparatory treatment only as regards the character and quantity of drink taken. The packs and diet of the preparatory treatment are continued during the strict treatment.

The strict treatment is begun by one whole day

of abstinence from wine-drinking. On the second day the habitual wine and rolls are taken. On the third day a morning glass of hot wine is sipped, and rolls eaten. In the afternoon one glass of hot wine is sipped, and then about one whole bottle of cold wine is sipped, whilst rolls are eaten. In the evening one glass of hot wine is sipped, and rolls eaten.

Treatment in Nervous Diseases.—In these cases the treatment is largely soothing, stimulation being approached by slow degrees. From three to six weeks the drinks may be barley-gruel and sugared water alternately. Then from three to six weeks more hot or cold water with wine. Then one day of abstinence is followed by a drinking day, and the wine is by degrees taken purer until the full treatment is attained.

The strict treatment arouses, perhaps many times during its course, a crisis in the body, with fever and perhaps acute local symptoms.

The preparatory treatment is then returned to, and the wine-drinking is omitted.

Period of Rest.—After some weeks of the strict treatment, the patient, by acquiring a keen appetite and good spirits, and by exhibiting a clean tongue, earns a period of rest of from one to two weeks' duration.

During this period of rest (1) a wet trunk-pack is substituted for the whole pack at night; (2) a

SCHROTH'S CURHAUS AT LINDEWIESE.

To face p. 184.

cup of cocoa or coffee is given for breakfast; (3) white meats, poultry or game, fresh vegetables and cooked fruits, are given for mid-day dinner, and half a bottle of wine with dry biscuits in the afternoon; (4) during the second week a light luncheon is given, with the object of keeping the dinner smaller. All meals must be strictly moderate in quantity. Nothing else is allowed except dry bread.

After a fortnight, or sooner, should the appetite diminish, or other discomfort arise, the strict treatment is resumed.

The object of this period of rest is to build up and reinvigorate the body, so that it will be better able to bear a further course of strict treatment if necessary.

Such is a bird's-eye view of the treatment pursued by Schroth during a period of fifty years. Invalids coming for the cure from all parts of the world is, to say the least, a fair indication that the remedies employed are attended with some success.

Dr. Schroth's treatment is adopted by eminent medical men in various parts of Europe. As a matter of course I do not include the medical men in England, Ireland, and Scotland, inasmuch as it would be *infra dig.* on their part to recognise such " quackery " as Dr. Schroth's method of dealing with their refuse. Individually, I am an eclectic so far as remedial measures are concerned; con-

sequently I am pleased to recognise every innovation that is calculated to ameliorate human
suffering. Being actuated by these principles, I
have made it my business to look into everything
that turns up pertaining to medical remedies that
have been developed either by accident or by scientific investigation.

About twenty-five years ago a gentleman called
at my establishment to see if he could have wet-
sheet packs according to Dr. Schroth's method.

The instructions were as follows : To be packed
in two suitable sized wet-sheets, well wrung out of
cold water ; fasting for three or four hours, followed
by a dry-sheet rub ; and to drink a small bottle of
white wine immediately after each pack.

This gentleman was suffering from septicæmia
of syphilitic nature ; he had ten applications, and
the improvement in the patient was marked. On
leaving, he declared that he had spent a fortune
in seeking for relief, adding that the ten packs,
together with the diet, had done him more good
than all previous remedies he had been under, and
as a result he had made up his mind to go to
Lindewiese to complete his cure.

This case made such a profound impression on
my mind that I was determined to visit Schroth's
establishment when an opportunity occurred, and
in 1895 I visited the place, and was very much
gratified with what I saw.

RECENT HYDROPATHY

It should be borne in mind that the Graefenberg and Lindewiese establishments are conducted very differently from the way in which our fashionable hydros are in this country. The major portion of the visitors are medical men's refuse from all parts of the globe, who flock there for treatment as a last resource, having been given up as incurable, and I have it from very good authority that a majority of those who undergo the treatment return home cured.

I think my readers will agree with me that it is a rather curious anomaly that so-called quackery has to come to the rescue of legalized medicine in the manner I have described.

*　　　*　　　*　　　*　　　*

In order to show the wide interest aroused by Priessnitz's work during his lifetime, I give in the next chapter a list of English works on and relating to hydropathy published between 1820 and 1850, and also lists of hydropathic authors in other languages during the same period.

CHAPTER XIII

HYDROPATHIC BOOKS

English Works : 1820—1850.

CLARKE (SIR ARTHUR). "An Essay on Warm, Cold, and Vapour-Bathing, with Observations on Sea-Bathing, Diseases of the Skin, Bilious Liver Complaints, and Dropsy." Fifth edition. London : printed for Henry Colburn and Co., and sold by John Cumming, and at the Public Baths. Dublin, 1820. 8vo., pp. xii, 232.

"Cursory Remarks on Bathing," to which are added observations on Sir Arthur Clarke's "Essay on Bathing." London : printed for T. Boys, 7, Ludgate Hill, 1820. 8vo., pp. 58.

Elliott (R.). "Dissertation on Cold Bathing." New York, 1821.

Bacon (—). "On Cold Applications." Philadelphia, 1822.

Mahomed (S. D.). "Shampooing ; or, Benefits Resulting from the Use of the Indian Medicated

Vapour-Bath . . . the Use of the Warm Bath in Comparison with Steam or Vapour-Bathing." Brighton: printed by E. H. Creasy, 1822. 8vo., pp. 134.—Third edition. Brighton: printed by William Fleet, *Herald* Office, 1838. 8vo., pp. xvi, 198.

Hunt (—). "Dissertation on Cold Applications." Philadelphia, 1824.

Dewees (W. P.). "A Treatise on the Physical and Medical Treatment of Children." London, 1826. (B. M.)

Syking (G. A.). "On the Effects of Drinking Cold Water." Philadelphia, 1826.

Blackwell (—). "On the Morbid Effects of Drinking Cold Water." Philadelphia, 1829.

Culverwell (R. J.). "A Practical Treatise on Bathing." London: published by the author, Founders' Hall Court, Lothbury, 1829. 8vo., pp. xvi, 248. (R. M.)

Donnellan (M.). "Dissertation on the Effects of Cold." Philadelphia, 1829.

Parks (—). "On the Effects of Cold." Diss, Philadelphia, 1829.

Bell (John). "On Baths and Mineral Waters." In two parts: Part I., "A Full Account of the Hygienic and Curative Powers of Cold, Tepid, Warm, Hot, and Vapour-Baths, and of Sea-Bathing." Part II., "Mineral Springs." Philadelphia, 1831.

Smith (Th.) " On Inflammation." Philadelphia, 1831.

Waring (J.). "On the Effects of Drinking Cold Water in Warm Weather." New York, 1831.

Whitlaw (Chas.). "A Treatise on the Causes and Effects of Inflammation, Fever, Cancer, Scrofula, and Nervous Affections, together with Remarks on the Specific Action of His Patent Medicated Vapour-Bath, and Rules for Diet and Regimen." London, 1831.

Edwards (W. F.). "On the Influence of Physical Agents on Life." Translated from the French by Dr. Hodgkin and Dr. Fisher. London, 1832. (B. M.)

Balbirnie (J.). " The Pathology and Treatment of the Functional Disorders and Organic Alterations of the Uterus and its Appendages, with a Series of New Cases Illustrating the Superior Efficacy of an Exclusive Water-Practice." London, 1836. (Another edition in 1846.)

Johnson (E.). " Letters to Brother John ; or, Life, Health, and Disease." London, 1837. (B. M.) (Many later editions.)

Wilson (Jas.). "A Practical Treatise on the Curative Effects of Simple and Medicated Vapour," etc. London, 1837. 8vo., pp. xii, 146 ; 2 plates.

Culverwell (R. J.). "Hints on Bathing, containing a Brief Exposition of the Medical Efficacy and Salubrity of the Warm, Vapour, Shampooing, Sulphur, and Shower-Baths." London, 1838.

Wright (M. B.). "A Lecture on the Physiological and Therapeutical Uses of Water, Delivered to the Students of the Ohio Medical College at the Opening of the Session of 1839-40." Cincinnati, 1839. 8vo.

Hall (Marshall). "On the Diseases and Derangements of the Nervous System." London, 1841. (Chapter VI.) (B. M.)

Abdy (E. S.). "The Water-Cure. Cases of Disease Cured by Cold Water." Translated from the German, with remarks addressed to people of common-sense. London, 1842. (B. M.)

Claridge (R. T.). "Hydropathy; or, the Cold-Water Cure as Practised by Vincent Priessnitz at Graefenberg, Silesia, Austria." London: J. Madden and Co., 1842. 8vo., pp. 318; 1 plate.

Freeman (J.). "Medical Reflections on the Water-Cure." London, 1842. (B. M.)

Graeter (F.). "Hydriatics; or, a Manual of the Water-Cure, especially as Practised by V. Priessnitz in Graefenberg." Compiled and translated from the writings of C. Munde, Dr. Oertel, Dr. B. Hirschel, and other eyewitnesses and practitioners. New York, 1842. (B. M.)

Gully (J. M.). "The Simple Treatment of Disease deduced from the Methods of Expectancy and Revulsion. . . ." London: J. Churchill, 1842. 12mo., pp. ii, viii, 198. (R. M.).

Priessnitz (Vincenz). "The Cold-Water Cure: its Principles, Theory, and Practice, with Hints for its Self-Application, and a Full Account of the Wonderful Cures Performed by it at Graefenberg . . . by the Inventor, V. Priessnitz." London, 1842. (B. M.)

Schlemmer (C. V.). "Hydropathy. The Cold-Water Cure of Diseases: its Philosophy and Fact. With Cases, proving how certainly this System Benefits the Afflicted." In two Lectures: (1) For the Healthy; (2) For the Sick. Translated from the German of Mr. C. V. Schlemmer, formerly conductor of the first hydropathic establishment in England, opened December, 1841, at Ham Common, Surrey; at present sub-director in the hydropathic establishment at Graefenberg House, Stanstead Bury, near Hertford. Price 1s. London: Madden and Co., Leadenhall Street; and Hatchard and Son, Piccadilly, 1842. 8vo., pp. 34. (B. M.)

Weatherhead (G. H.). "On the Hydropathic Cure of Gout." London, 1842. (B. M.)

Wilson (James). "The Water-Cure. A Practical Treatise on the Cure of Diseases by Water, Air, Exercise, and Diet: being a New Mode of restoring Injured Constitutions to Robust Health, for the Radical Cure of Dyspeptic, Nervous, and Liver Complaints, Tic-Douloureux, Gout, and

Rheumatism, Scrofula, Syphilis, and their Consequences, Diseases Peculiar to Women and Children, Fevers, Inflammations," etc. Fourth edition. London: John Churchill, 1842. 8vo., pp. xxx, 202. (R. M.)

Beamish (R.). "The Cold-Water Cure . . . to which are added some Useful Hints . . . together with a Notice of the Dipsopathic System of Schrott at Lindiviese." Second edition. London, 1843. (B. M.)

Beamish (R.). "Approximate Rationale of the Cold-Water Cure as Practised by V. Priessnitz at Graefenberg in Silesia, with an Account of Cases successfully treated at Prestbury near Cheltenham." London, 1843. (B. M.)

Courtney (Ab.). "The Water-Cure: its Safety and Rationality." London, 1843. (B. M.)

Graham (T. J.). "A Few Pages on Hydropathy, or the Cold-Water System." London, 1843. (B. M.)

Graham (T. J.). "The Cold-Water System, an Essay Exhibiting the Real Merits and Most Safe . . . Employment of this Excellent System in Indigestion, Costiveness, Asthma, Cough," etc. London, 1843. (B. M.)

Heathcote (G. H.). "Some Observations on the Cold-Water Treatment as Witnessed at Graefenberg." London, 1843. (B. M.)

Johnson (E.). "Hydropathy. The Theory,

Principles and Practice of the Water-Cure."
London, 1843. (B. M.) Third thousand. London:
Simpkin and Co., 1846. 8vo., pp. 194.

Johnson (E.). "The Water-Cure. A Lecture
on the Principles of Hydropathy." London, 1843.
(B. M.)

Scudamore (Sir Charles). "A Medical Visit
to Graefenberg, in . . . 1843, for the Purpose of
Investigating the Merits of the Water-Cure Treatment." London, 1843. (B. M.)

Smethurst (Thos.). "Hydrotherapia; or, the
Water-Cure. . . . To which is added a Description of Graefenberg and the System there. . . .
Together with a Short Sketch of the History of
the Water-Cure . . . and Remarks on Sea-Bathing." London, 1843. (B. M.)

Wilson (James). "The Water-Cure. Stomach
Complaints and Drug Diseases, their Causes, Consequences and Cure by Water, Air, Exercise and
Diet. With an Engraving of Napoleon in the
Second Stage of Cancer of the Stomach. To
which is Appended two Letters to Dr. Hastings,
of Worcester, on the Results of the Water-Cure
at Malvern. . . ." London : J. Churchill, Princes
Street, Soho, 1843. 8vo., pp. xvi, 130. (R. M.)

Wilson (James) and Gully (J. M.). "The
Dangers of the Water-Cure and its Efficacy
Examined," etc. London : Cunningham and
Mortimer. 1843. 12mo., pp. xiv, 186.

Wilson (J.) and Gully (J. M.). "A Prospectus of the Water-Cure Establishment at Malvern under the Management of J. W., M.D., and J. M. G., M.D. London : Cunningham and Mortimer, 1843. 12mo., pp. iv, 32. (R. M.)

Feldmann (J. E.). "Theory and Practice of Hydropathy . . . Physiologically and Pathologically Reviewed and Compared with the old Medical Treatment." Dublin, 1843. 8vo. (B. M.)

Martin (E. G.). "Principles of Cold-Water Treatment of Diseases, and its Application." London, 1843. 8vo. (B. M.)

Weeding (Samuel). "The Wet Sheet : Addressed to the Medical Men of England. Cases Illustrative of the Powerful and Curative Effect of the Wet Sheet," etc. London [Ryde, printed], 1843. 8vo. (B. M.)

Claridge (R. T.). "Facts and Evidences in Support of Hydropathy." London : J. Madden and Co., 1844. 8vo. 1s. 6d.

Martin (E. G.). "Water-Treatment of Gout and Rheumatism : the Reasons of its Failure in these cases ; with Remarks on the Injurious Effects of Iodine." London [Weymouth, printed], 1844. 8vo. (B. M.)

Graham (R. Hay). "Graefenberg ; or, A True Report of the Water-Cure, with an Account of its Antiquity." London, 1844 : Longman and Co., 1844. 8vo., pp. iv, 232.

Greaves (John), *Editor*. " The History of Cold Bathing, both Ancient and Modern, by Sir John Floyer, Knt., and Dr. Edward Baynard. First published about the year 1702. Manchester : Republished by J. Gadsby, Newall's Buildings. London : R. Groombridge, 5, Paternoster Row, 1844. Price 1s. 8vo., pp. 108. A reprint of the fifth edition of 1722. (R. M.)

King (John). " Observations on Hydropathy ; or, the Cold-Water Cure, Elucidated by some Remarkable Cases, as Witnessed by the Author during his Residence at Graefenberg, Silesian Austria." London, 1844 (?). (B. M.)

Lee (Edwin). " The Cold-Water Cure." Reprinted with additions from the last edition of " The Baths of Germany." London, 1844. (B. M.)

Shew (Joel). "Handbook of Hydropathy." New York : Wiley and Putnam, 1844. 12mo., pp. 144.

Shew (Joel). " Facts in Hydropathy, or the Water-Cure ; a Collection of Cases, with Details of Treatment, showing the Safest and Most Effectual Known Means to be Used in Gout, Rheumatism, Indigestion, Hypochondriasis, Fevers, Consumption, etc., from various Authors." New York : Burgess, Stringer and Co., 1844. 12mo., pp. 108.

Weiss (John). " The Handbook of Hydropathy ; with an Appendix on the Best Mode of

Forming Hydros." London : J. Madden and Co., 1844. 8vo., pp. xii, 438.

Wilson (James). " The Practice of the Water-Cure, with Authenticated Evidence of its Efficacy and Safety." Part I. London, 1844. (B. M.)

The Water-Cure Journal. Edited by Joel Shew. New York, 1845-49.

Balbirnie (J.). " The Philosophy of the Water-Cure ; a Development of the True Principles of Health and Longevity." Bath : Binns and Goodwin. London : Simpkin and Co., 1845. 12mo., pp. xl, 386.

Bodwell (J. C.). " Remarks on the Water-Cure." Weymouth, 1845.

Courtney (Abraham). " Hydropathy Defended by Facts ; or, the Cold-Water Cure Proved to be as Safe in Practice as it is Rational in Theory." London, 1845 (?).

Horsell (W.) " The Board of Health and Longevity ; or; Hydropathy for the People : Consisting of Plain Observations on Drugs, Diet, Water, Air, Exercise, etc." London : Houlston and Stoneman, 1845. 16mo., pp. 254.

Mayo (Herbert). " The Cold-Water Cure, its Use and Misuse Examined." London, 1845. (B. M.)

Wright (H. C.) " Six Months at Graefenberg ; with Conversations in the Saloon on Non-resistance and other Subjects. . . ." London : C. Gilpin, 1845. 8vo., pp. viii, 358. (R. M.)

VINCENT PRIESSNITZ

Bulwer-Lytton (E. G. E. L.), *Baron Lytton.*
" Confessions of a Water-Patient ; in a Letter to
W. H. Ainsworth. London, 1846. (B. M.)

Bushnan (J. S.). "Observations on Hydro-
pathy, with an Account of the Principal Cold-
Water Establishments of Germany." Berlin : A.
Asher and Co. Frankfort : C. Jugel. Neuwied :
A. G. van der Beck. London : J. Churchill, 1846.
12mo., pp. xii, 188. (B. M.)

Gully (J. M.). "The Water-Cure in Chronic
Disease." London, 1846. (B. M.) (Second edition,
1847. Third edition, 1850. Fourth edition, 1851.
Fifth edition, 1856. Sixth edition, 1859.)

Lee (Edwin). "Hydropathy and Homœopathy
Impartially Appreciated, with an Appendix of
Notes Illustrative of the Influence of the Mind
on the Body." The third editions combined.
London : Churchill, 1847. 12mo. (B. M.)

Feldmann (J. E.). "Cold-Water Cure, and
Results of Twenty Years' Medical Practice."
London, 1847. 8vo. (B. M.)

Ross (David). "Atmopathy and Hydropathy ;
or, How to Prevent and Cure Diseases by the
Application of Steam and Water." London
[Ipswich, printed]: Simpkin, 1848. 16mo. 2s. 6d.
(B. M.)

Johnson (Ed.). "Results of Hydropathy; or,
Constipation not a Disease of the Bowels; Indigestion not a Disease of the Stomach; with an

Exposition of the True Nature and Cause of these Ailments, explaining the reason why they are certainly Cured by the Hydropathic Treatment," etc. London : Simpkin and Co. Ipswich : J. M. Burton, 1846. 8vo., pp. viii, 268. (B. M.)

Lane (R. J.). " Life at the Water-Cure ; or, A Month at Malvern, a Diary. To which is added the Sequel." London : Longmans, 1846. 8vo., pp. xiv, 386.

Lee (Edwin). " The Baths of Germany . . . and an Appendix on the Cold-Water Cure." Third reissue. London, 1846. (B. M.)

Gibbs (John), *of Camberwell.* " Letters from Graefenberg, in . . . 1843-46, with the Report and Extracts from the Correspondence of the Enniscorthy Hydropathic Society." London : C. Gilpin, 1847. 8vo., pp. xxviii, 280.

Hartshorne (H.) " Water *versus* Hydropathy ; or, An Essay on Water, and its True Relations to Medicine." Philadelphia : L. P. Smith, 1847. 8vo., pp. 132. (R. M.)

Shew (Joel). " The Water-Cure Manual . . . with Descriptions of Diseases and the Hydropathic Means to be Employed Therein." New York, 1847. (B. M.)

Veteran (By a). " Hints to the Sick, the Lame, and the Lazy ; or, Passages in the Life of a Hydropathist." London, 1847.

The Water-Cure Journal. Edited by J. M.

Gully. London : No. 1, August, 1847; No. 38, September, 1850.

Balbirnie (J.). " Curability of Consumption ; with Cases . . . Prospectus of the Water . . . Cure Practised at Cheltenham." London, 1848. (B. M.)

Forbes (Sir John). " Review of Hydropathy, or the Water-Cure." From the *London Quarterly Journal*, October, 1848. (Troy, New York). Published by Dr. W. A. Hamilton, 1848. (B. M.)

Macleod (Wm.). " The Treatment of Small-Pox, Measles, Scarlet Fever, etc., by the Water-Cure and Homœopathy." Manchester, 1848. (B. M.)

Meeker (C. H.). " Miscellanies to the Graefenberg Water-Cure ; or, A Demonstration of the Advantages of the Hydropathic Method of Curing Diseases as compared with the Medical." Translated (from the German of J. H. Rausse) by C. H. Meeker. New York : published under the direction of Drs. Pierson and Meeker, 1848. 12mo., pp. xvi, 262. (B. M.)

" The Water-Cure in America ; 220 Cases of Various Diseases Treated with Water by Drs. Wesselhoefft, Shew, Bedertha, Schieferdecker, and others." Edited by a Water-Patient. Second edition. New York and London, 1848. (B. M.)

Blackie (J. S.). " The Water-Cure in Scotland ; Five Letters from Dunoon, originally published in the *Aberdeen Herald*. Aberdeen, 1849. (B. M.)

Claridge (R. T.) "Cholera : its Prevention and Cure by Hydropathy; with Observations on the Treatment of Colic, Diarrhœa, and Dysentery." London, 1849. (B. M.)

Claridge (R. T.). "Every Man his own Doctor, the Cold Water, Tepid Water, and Friction Cure, as Applicable to every Disease to which the Human Frame is subject, and also to the Cure of Disease in Horses and Cattle." London, 1849. (B. M.)

Francke (H. F.). "Outlines of a New Theory of Disease Applied to Hydropathy." Translated from the German by R. Baikie. London: Longman and Co., 1849. 8vo., pp. viii, 320.

Johnson (E.). "The Domestic Practice of Hydropathy." London, 1849. (B. M.) (Many later editions.)

Nichols (Mrs. M. S. G.). "Experience in Water-Cure; a Familiar Exposition of the Principles and Results of Water-Treatment in the Cure of Acute and Chronic Diseases Illustrated by Numerous Cases in the Practice of the Author," etc. New York, 1849. (B. M.)

Schieferdecker (C. C.). "Short Essay on the Invariably Successful Treatment of Cholera with Water." Philadelphia, 1849. (B. M.)

Shew (Joel). "The Cholera: its Causes, Prevention and Cure ; showing the Inefficacy of Drug-Treatment and the Superiority of the Water-Cure in this Disease." New York, 1849. (B. M.)

Shew (Joel). "The Water-Cure in Pregnancy and Childbirth, with Cases Showing the Remarkable Effects of Water in Mitigating the Pains . . . of the Parturient State." New York, 1849. (B. M.)

Claridge (R. T.). "Familiar Guide to Hydropathy." London: J. Madden and Co., 1849. 8vo. 2s. 6d.

Bell (John). "Dietetical and Medical Hydrology. A Treatise on Baths; including Cold, Sea, Warm, Hot, Vapour, Gas, and Mud Baths; also on the Watery Regimen, Hydropathy and Pulmonary Inhalation; with a Description of Bathing in Ancient and Modern Times." Philadelphia, 1850.

Hunter (Robert). "Hydrotherapeutics; or, A Treatise on the Water-Cure." Toronto, 1850 (?).

Johnson (E.). "The History, Claims, and Prospects of Hydropathy." London, 1850. (B.M.)

Johnson (E.). "The Hydropathic Treatment of Diseases Peculiar to Women." London, 1850. (B. M.)

Johnson (H. F.). "Researches into the Effects of Cold Water upon the Healthy Body, to Illustrate its Action in Disease, in a Series of Experiments Performed by the Author upon Himself and Others." Manchester, 1850. (B. M.)

Nichols (T. L.). "Introduction to the Water-Cure." New York, 1850 (?).

Nichols (Thos. L.). "The Curse Removed. A

Statement of Facts Respecting the Efficacy of the Water-Cure in the Treatment of Uterine Diseases, and the Removal of the Pains and Perils of Pregnancy and Childbirth." New York: Office of the *Water-Cure Journal,* 1850. 12mo., pp. 20.

Rausse (J. H.). "Errors of Physicians and Others in the Practice of the Water-Cure." New York, 1850 (?).

Shew (J.). "Hydropathy, or the Water-Cure: its Principles, Processes, and Mode of Treatment," etc. Fourth edition. New York, 1850. 12mo., pp. 360. Vol. I. of the Water-Cure Library.

Trall (R. T.) "Hydropathy for the People." New York, 1850 (?).

The following works I have failed to find fuller information about:

Dr. Preshaw. "Wet Sheet."

Mrs. Shew. "Hydropathy for Ladies."

Mr. Wilmot. "Tribute."

APPENDIX

AUTHORS OF ENGLISH WORKS, 1820-50.

Abdy, E. S., 1842.
Bacon, —, 1822.
Balbirnie, J., 1845-48.
Beamish, R., 1843.
Bell, J., 1831-50.
Blackie, J. S., 1849.
Blackwell, —, 1829.
Bodwell, J. C., 1845.
Bulwer-Lytton, E.G.E.L., 1846.
Bushnan, J. S., 1846.
Claridge, R. T., 1842-4-9.
Clarke, Sir A., 1820.
Courtney, Ab., 1843-45.
Culverwell, R. J., 1829-38.
'Cursory Remarks,' 1820.
Dewees, W. P., 1826.
Donnellan, M., 1829.
Elliott, R., 1821.
Edwards, W. F., 1832.
Feldmann, J. E., 1843-47.
Forbes, J., 1848.
Francke, H. F., 1849.
Freeman, J., 1842.
Gibbs, J., 1847.

Græter, F., 1842.
Graham, T. J., 1843.
Graham, R. H., 1844.
Greaves, J., 1844.
Gully, J. M., 1842-50.
Hall, M., 1841.
Hartshorne, H., 1847.
Heathcote, G. H., 1843.
Horsell, W., 1845.
Hunt, —, 1824.
Hunter, R., 1850.
Johnson, E., 1837-50.
Johnson, H. F., 1850.
King, J., 1844.
Lane, R. J., 1846.
Lee, E., 1844-6-7.
Macleod, W., 1848.
Mahomed, S. D., 1822-38.
Martin, E. G., 1843-44.
Mayo, H., 1845.
Meeker, C. H., 1848.
Nichols, M. S. G., 1849.
Nichols, S. L., 1850.
Parks, —, 1829.
Priessnitz, V., 1842.

APPENDIX

Rausse, J.'H., 1848-50.
Ross, D., 1848.
Schieferdecker, C. C., 1849.
Schlemmer, C. V., 1842.
Scudamore, C., 1843.
Shew, J., 1844-50.
Smith, Th., 1831.
Smethurst, T., 1843.
Syking, G. A., 1826.
Trall, R. T., 1850.
'Veteran,' 1847.
Waring, J., 1831.

Water Cure Journal, London, 1847-50.
Water Cure Journal, New York, 1845-50.
Weatherhead, G. H., 1842.
Weeding, S., 1843.
Weiss, J., 1844.
Wesselhoefft, —, 1848.
Whitlaw, C., 1831.
Wilson, J., 1837-44.
Wright, M. B., 1839.
Wright, H. C., 1845.

AUTHORS OF GERMAN WORKS, 1820-50.

Amon, E. O., 1838.
Baumann, G. A., 1845.
Bayshoffer, C. Th., 1837.
Beck, V. W., 1838.
Beckstein, —, 1834-37.
Bergmann, A. L., 1838.
Bicking, F. A., 1842.
Brand, T., 1835.
Brandis, J. D., 1833.
Braune, —, 1843.
Buchner, J. B., 1845.
Bürckner, —, 1841.
Caspar, J. B., 1832.
Classen, H., 1840.
Cohn, S. D., 1843.
Colomb, M. von, 1850.
Dahne, R. F., 1821.
Decken-Himmelreich, L. von der, 1845.
Dietrich, E. C. V., 1840.
Doering, —, 1836.
Doussin-Doubreil, J. L., 1828.

Dzondi, C. H., 1825.
Ehrenberg, H., 1840.
Erhard, —, 1824.
Erismann, A., 1847.
Fabricius, —, 1834.
Flittner, C. G., 1822.
Fraenkel, L., 1840-42.
Froelich, A. von, 1823-45.
Granichstädten, S. M., 1837.
Gross, J. B., 1836-47.
Hahn, J. S., 1838.
Hahn, Th., 1850.
Hallmann, Ed., 1844-50.
Hancocke, J., 1834.
Heine, J. G., 1835.
Held-Ritt, E. von, 1837.
Helmenstreit, —, 1839.
Hermann, —, 1835.
Herzog, A., 1836.
Hirschel, B., 1840.
Hlawaczek, E., 1837.
Hoppe, J., 1840.

Horner, —, 1840.
Husemann, G., 1837.
Kahl, C., 1848.
Kapp, E., 1850.
Keyser, —, 1841.
Kirchmayer, A., 1838.
Klencke, P. F. H., 1840.
Knolz, J. J., 1834.
Kobbe, T. von, 1841.
Kock, C. F., 1831.
Kock, K. A., 1838.
Kollert, —, 1837.
Krausse, W., 1842.
Krober, A. H., 1833.
Kuehn, A., 1841.
Kuerter, R., 1841-44.
Kurtz, T. E., 1835.
Landa, —, 1842.
Laube, H., —.
Leupoldt, J. M., 1842.
Mauthner von Mautstein, L. W., 1837.
Mayor, M. L., 1847.
Mediolanus, —, 1847.
Meissner, F. L., 1832.
Michalovits, —, 1842.
Möller, J. G., 1839.
Müller, F., 1832.
Müller, F. O. C., 1845.
Müller, J. O., 1840.
Munde, C., 1837-47.
Neumann, A. C., 1846.
Neumann, C. G., 1845-47.
Niedenfuehr, M. C., 1850.
Oertel, E. F. C., 1829-40.
Oxann, —, 1829.
Osiander, —, 1829.
Ott, F. A., 1845.
Parow, W., 1841-44.
Petri, —, 1841.

Plitt, H. O., 1845-47.
Putzer, J., 1847-50.
Raimann, F., 1844.
Raimund, J. K., 1845.
Rast, F. G. L., 1829-40.
Rausse, J. H., 1838-50.
Rechberg, —, 1841.
Reich, G. C., 1831.
Reider, J. E. von, 1831.
Reuss, J. I., 1831.
Richter, A., 1834.
Richter, C. A. W., 1838.
Rickauer, G. J., 1838.
Röber, E., 1845.
Roder, A., 1841.
Roetel, —, 1843-48.
Röver, —, 1832.
Rul, M., —.
Ruppricht, S., 1840.
Rust, J. N., 1832.
Sachs, L., 1849.
Sachs, S., 1845.
Sachs, J. J., 1838.
Schede, —, 1833.
Schenk, C., 1843.
Schmethurst, T., 1847.
Schnackenberg, —, 1841.
Schnaubert, H., 1840.
Schnitzlein, E., 1838.
Schreiber, D. G. M., 1842.
Schroth, J., 1846.
Schubert, F., 1840.
Selinger, J. E. M., 1841.
Seyfart, G., 1846.
Siebenhaar, F. J., 1831.
Sinogowitz, H. S., 1840.
Stark, A., 1844.
Stecher, —, 1840-44.
Steudel, E. G., 1842.

APPENDIX

Steudel, H., 1840.
Strahl, M., 1846.
Stuhlmann, —, 1850.
Tarani, F., 1841.
Vetter, F. G. A., 1840.
Vierordt, C., 1845.
Vogel, M. J., 1828-45.
Weber, B., 1847.

Weiss, J., 1844.
Wriskopf, H., 1847.
Wendt, J., 1830-44.
Wichmann, —, 1841.
Wulzinger, —, 1839.
Zipperlen, J. B., 1844-47.
Zoczek, C., 1836.
Zorzeck, —, 1831.

AUTHORS OF FRENCH WORKS, 1820-50.

Amussat, A. A., 1850.
Andral, G., 1836.
Bachelier, J., 1843.
Baldou, —, 1841.
Beley, C., 1833.
Beunaiche de la Corbière, J. B., 1839.
Bigel, J., 1840.
Busquet, P. F., 1849.
Chabot, —, 1830.
Chantelou, F., 1834.
Chapuis, J., 1844.
Corbel, S. J., 1837-45.
Delaveau, F. C., 1823.
Dieppedalle, L. F., 1844.
Dumay, C. S., 1830.
Duvard, J. M., 1834.
Edwards, Wm. F., 1824.
Engel, —, 1840.
Geoffroy, —, 1843.
Gillebert-Dhercourt, L. A., 1845.
Guillet, M. J. J. M., 1834.
Habets, —, 1842.
Heidenhain, H., 1842.
James, C., 1846.

Joannes, —, 1828.
Jolly, P., 1829.
Josse, —, 1835.
Legrand, —, 1843.
Lubansky, A., 1845-47.
Mayor, C., 1844.
Mayor, M. L., 1846.
Meglin, A., 1822.
Mestre, J. A., 1824.
Munde, C., 1842.
Pigeaire, J., 1842-47.
Poullain, —, 1842.
Raymond, V., 1840.
Rochoux, —, 1829.
Rouvière, —, 1823.
Rowe, —, 1824.
Sauvan, —, 1840.
Schedel, H. E., 1845.
Scoutetten, R. H. J., 1843-44.
Tanchou, S., 1821.
Van Housebrouck, —, 1841.
Van Swygenbooen, C., 1842.
Vidart, P., 1849.
Wertheim, L., 1840.

APPENDIX

AUTHORS OF LATIN WORKS, 1820-50.

Black, —, 1829.
Blaschka, J., 1842.
Bloch, H., 1839.
Breitenbücher, H., 1844.
Brüggemann, A. F., 1824.
Cocchi, B., 1829.
Folcieri, F., 1835.
Fraenkel, L., 1830.
Fuellkruss, C. F., 1843.
Gritzner, E. T., 1841.
Grünhut, J., 1842.
Guentha, G. B., 1844.
Harvey, J., 1828.
Henckel, W., 1828.
Heyck, J. H. G., 1836.
Jackson, G., 1823.
Karass, C., 1845.
Kier, A., 1830.
Kitzing, G., 1839.
Knie, J. A., 1833.
Kurinsky, J., 1829.
Laband, L., 1826.

Leinveber, F. G., 1843.
Lenaert, F. J., 1823.
Leonhardi, F. M., 1843.
Levin, L., 1846.
Lienard, C., 1826.
Lorinser, R., 1823.
Matiegka, F., 1835.
Meyer, P., 1822.
Müller, J., 1831.
Nolan, J., 1826.
Oertel, E. F. C., 1826.
Rothmann, F. L., 1823.
Sachs, A., 1825.
Schaforowsky, —, 1834.
Schmidt, T., 1847.
Stechern, A., 1842.
Stumpt, F. G., 1822.
Tremmel, E., 1836.
Wigand, —, 1829.
Wiselius, S. J., 1825.
Zimmermann, H. H. F., 1844.

AUTHORS OF WORKS IN OTHER LANGUAGES, 1820-50.

Ascholin, J., 1832.
Bertini, —, 1838.
Claridge, R. T., 1848.
Cocchi, A., 1824.
Egeberg, —, 1841.

Kolaczkowsky, A., 1840.
Lichtenthal, P., 1838.
Raymond, V., 1841.
Stummes, J., 1842.

INDEX

I. GENERAL

INDEX

II. NAMES

INDEX

III. PRIESSNITZ

THE END.

Wilkes and Co., Printers, 88, *Walworth Road, London, S.E.*

ERRATA.

Page 32, line 15, *for* " Sotzbeck ' *read* " Lotzbeck."

Page 32, line 17, *for* " G. H. O. Moor " *read* " J. H. O. Moore."

Page 48, line 19, *for* " Budamir " *read* " Budamér."

Page 49, line 14, *for* " Bochin " *read* " Boehm."

Page 67, line 15, *for* " Spinner " *read* " Sponner."

Page 134, line 22, *for* " Jäger " *read* " Jaeger."

Page 135, line 13, *for* " Buchelsdorf " *read* " Buechelsdorf."

Page 148, line 4, *for* " Neues " *read* " Neue."

Page 148, line 20, *for* " Grosses " *read* " Grosse."

Page 149, line 22, *for* " Hosann " *read* " Hosanu."

Page 149, line 23, *for* " Habschek " *read* " Hatschek."

Page 154, line 30, *for* " deutscher " *read* " deutschen."

Page 155, line 26, *for* " spiritze " *read* " spritze."

Page 176, line 25, *for* " Emanuel " *read* " Edouard."